T0297480

Scribner
1230 Avenue of the
Americas
New York, NY 10020

WHO'S GOT GAME?

The Lion or
the Mouse?

TONI & SLADE MORRISON
pictures by PASCAL LEMAITRE

This book is a work of fiction.
Names, characters, places, and incidents either are products of the author's imagination or are used fictitiously.
Any resemblance to actual events or locales or persons, living or dead, is entirely coincidental!

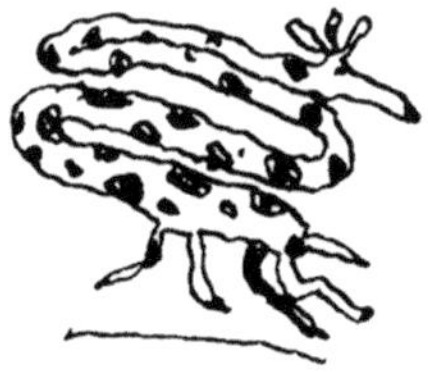

For INFORMATION regarding special discounts for bulk purchases, please contact Simon & Schuster Special Sales at 1-800-456-6798 or business@simonandschuster.com

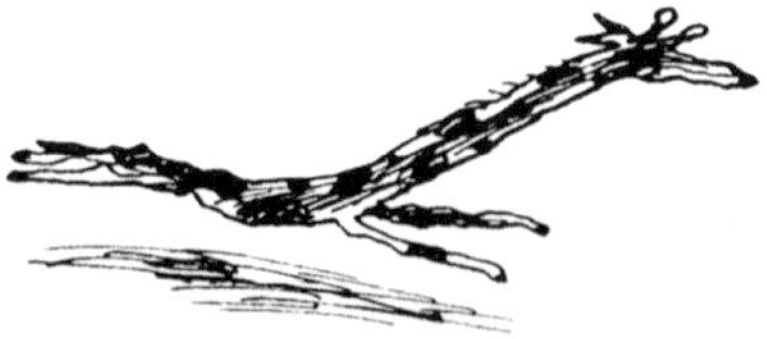

SCRIBNER and design are trademarks of Macmillan Library Reference USA, Inc., used under license by Simon & Schuster, the publisher of this work.

DESIGNED by Pascal Lemaitre; colors by P. Lemaitre & E. Phuon.

Manufactured in the United States of America.
10 9 8 7 6 5 4 3 2 1

Library of Congress Cataloging-in-Publication Data
Morrison, Toni.
    The lion or the mouse? / by Toni Morrison
                                and Slade Morrison;
        illustrated by Pascal Lemaitre.
    p. cm. — (Who's got game?)

    1. Aesop's fables — Adaptations. 2. Fables, American.
    I. Morrison, Slade. II. Lemaître, Pascal. III. Title.

    PS3563.O8749 L56 2003
    813'.54—dc21
                                        2002036451

    ISBN: 978-1-4767-9268-2

to Nidol
T.M.

to Kali-Ma
S.M.

to my dad.
P.L.

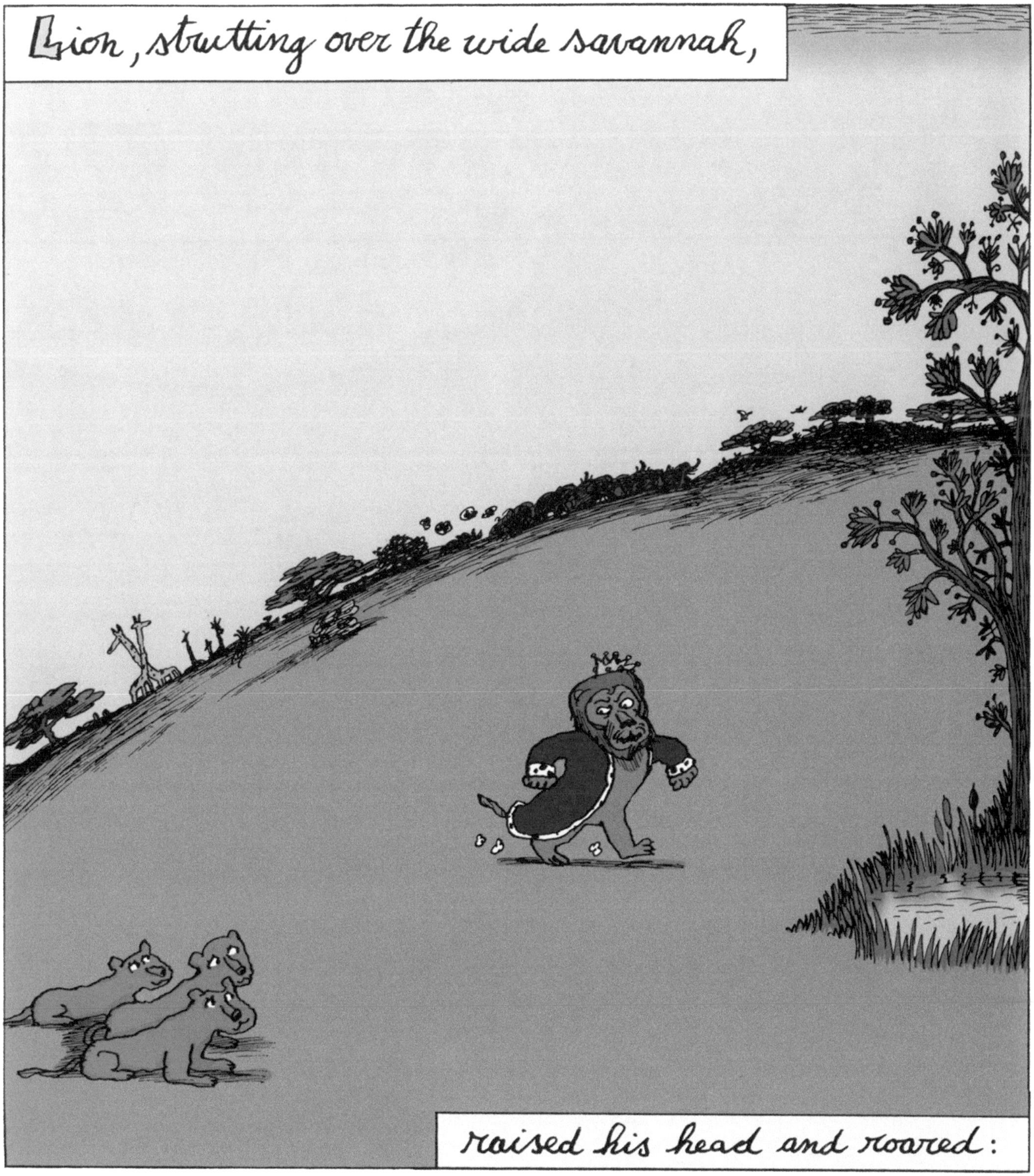
Lion, strutting over the wide savannah,
raised his head and roared:

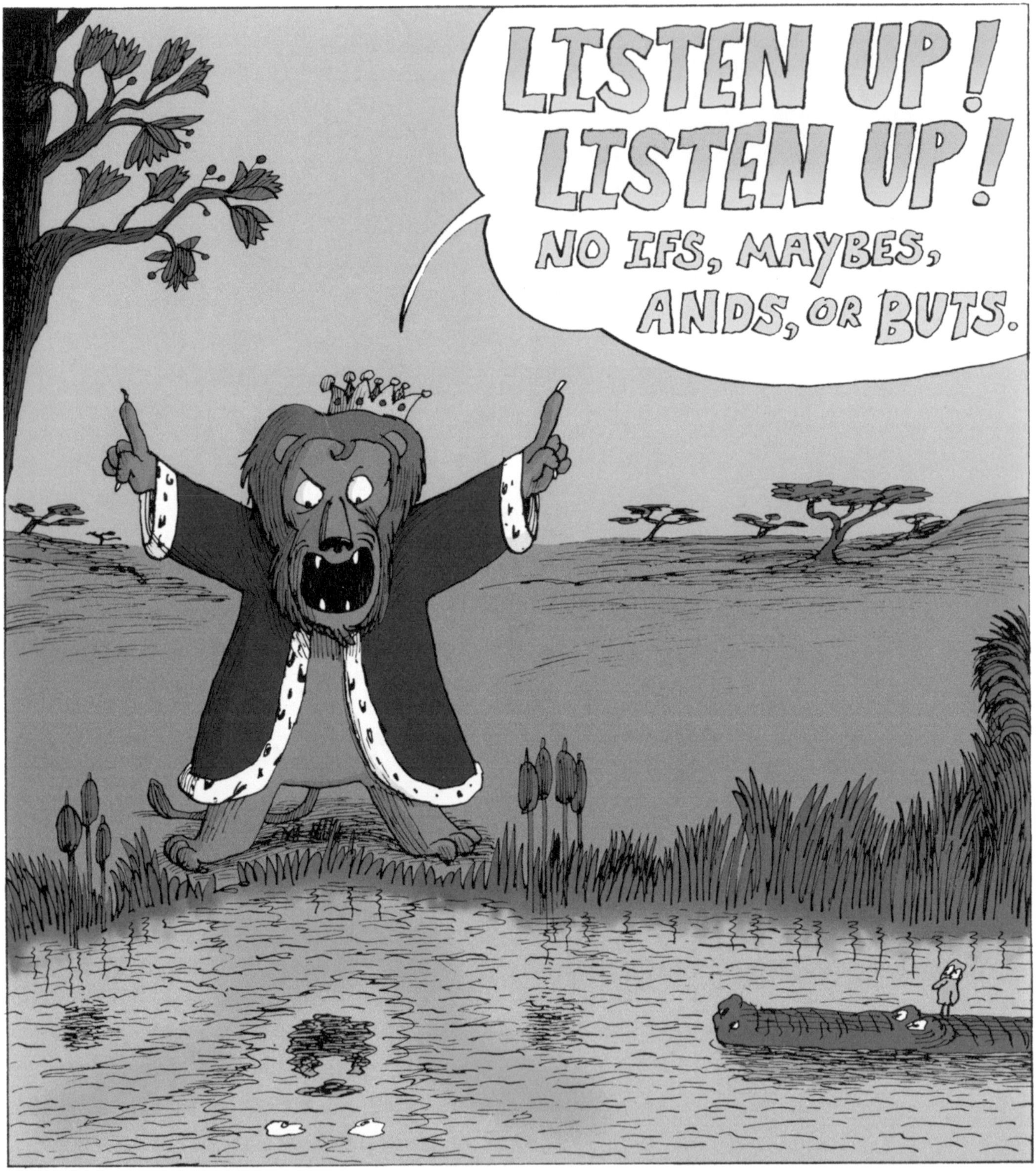
LISTEN UP! LISTEN UP!
NO IFS, MAYBES, ANDS, OR BUTS.

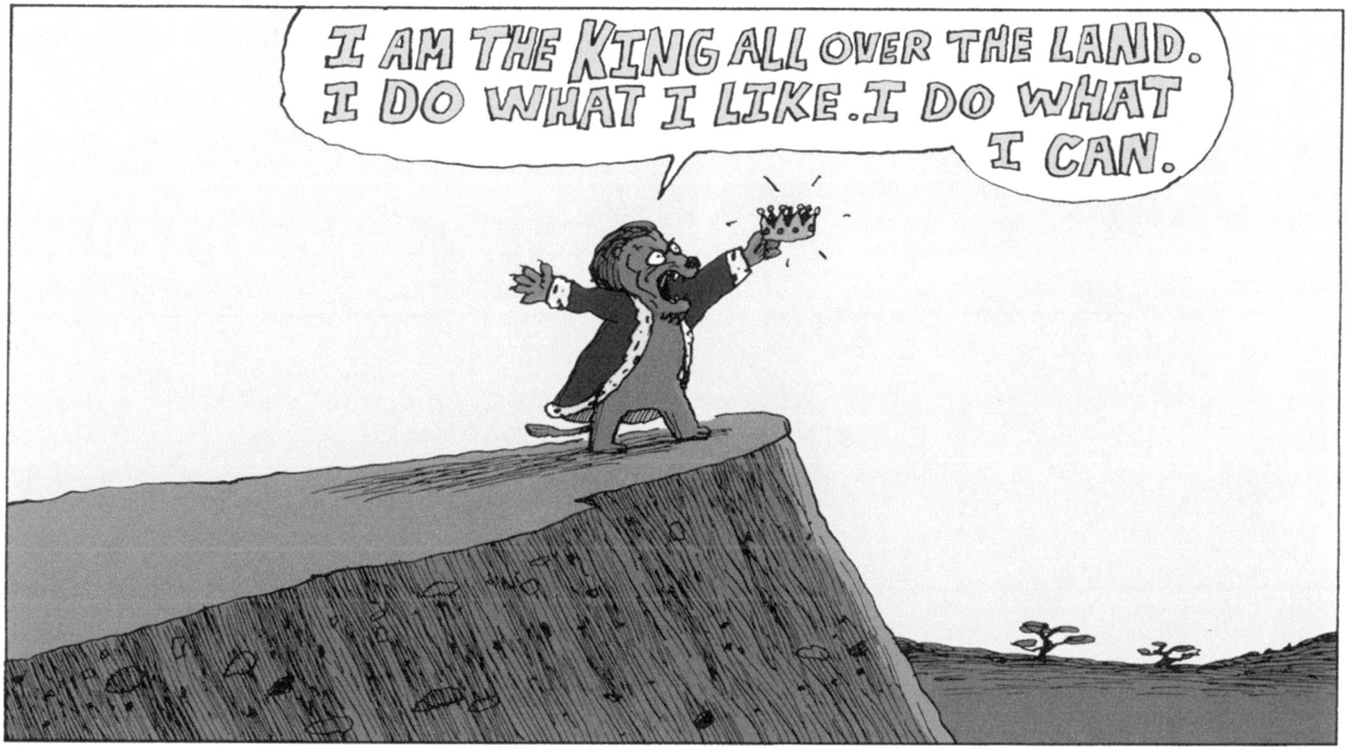
I AM THE KING ALL OVER THE LAND. I DO WHAT I LIKE. I DO WHAT I CAN.

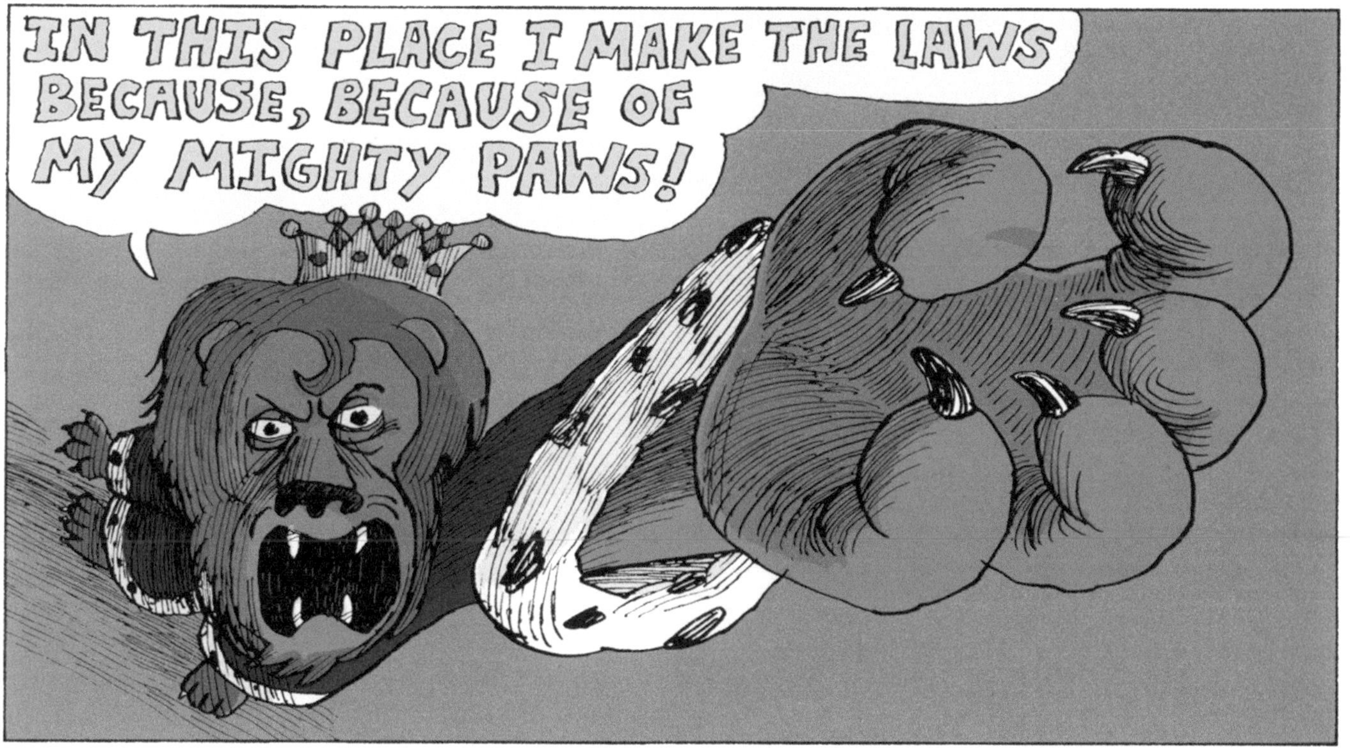
IN THIS PLACE I MAKE THE LAWS BECAUSE, BECAUSE OF MY MIGHTY PAWS!

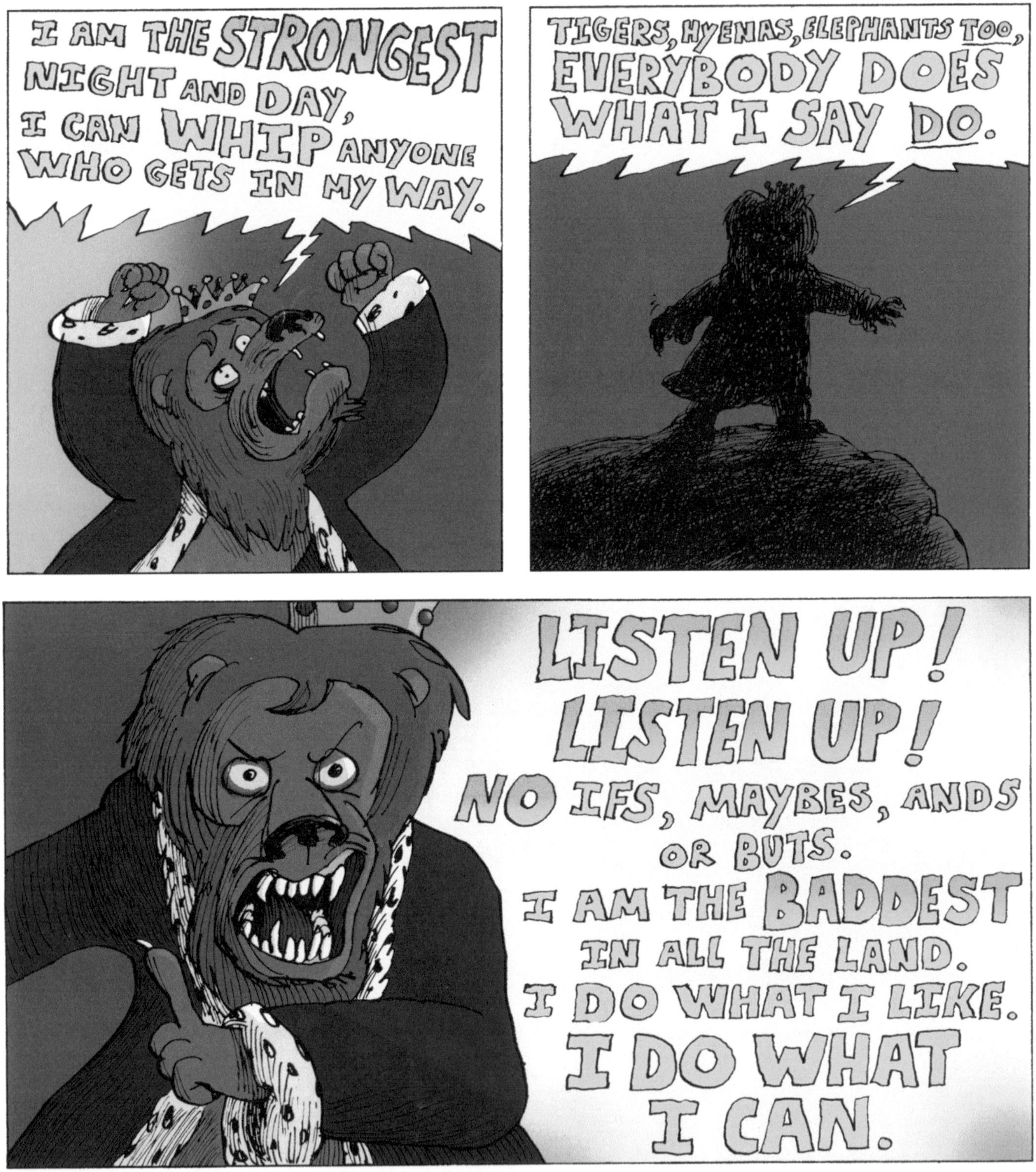
I AM THE STRONGEST NIGHT AND DAY, I CAN WHIP ANYONE WHO GETS IN MY WAY.
TIGERS, HYENAS, ELEPHANTS TOO, EVERYBODY DOES WHAT I SAY DO.
LISTEN UP! LISTEN UP! NO IFS, MAYBES, ANDS OR BUTS. I AM THE BADDEST IN ALL THE LAND. I DO WHAT I LIKE. I DO WHAT I CAN.

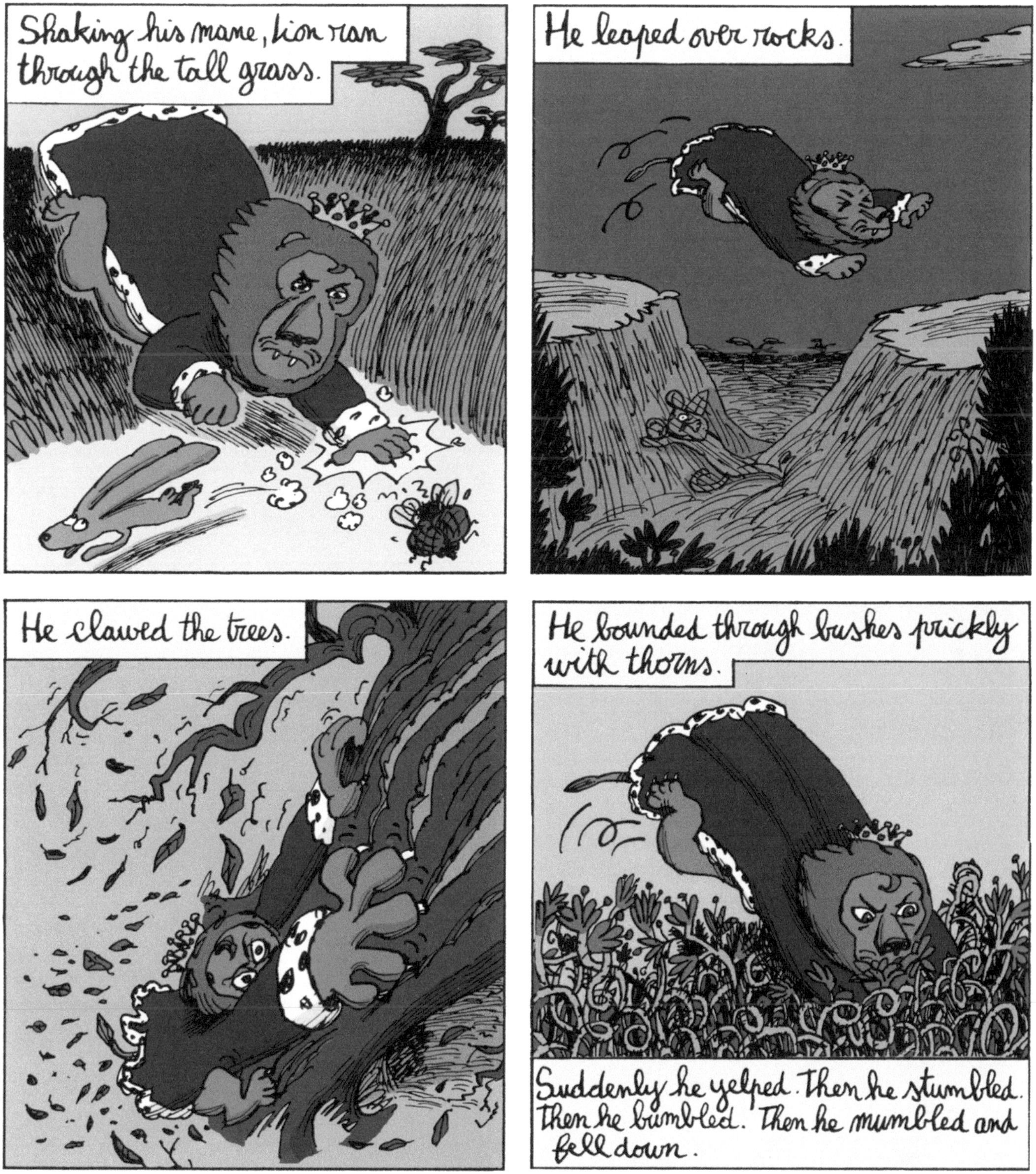
Shaking his mane, Lion ran through the tall grass.
He leaped over rocks.
He clawed the trees.
He bounded through bushes prickly with thorns.
Suddenly he yelped. Then he stumbled. Then he bumbled. Then he mumbled and fell down.

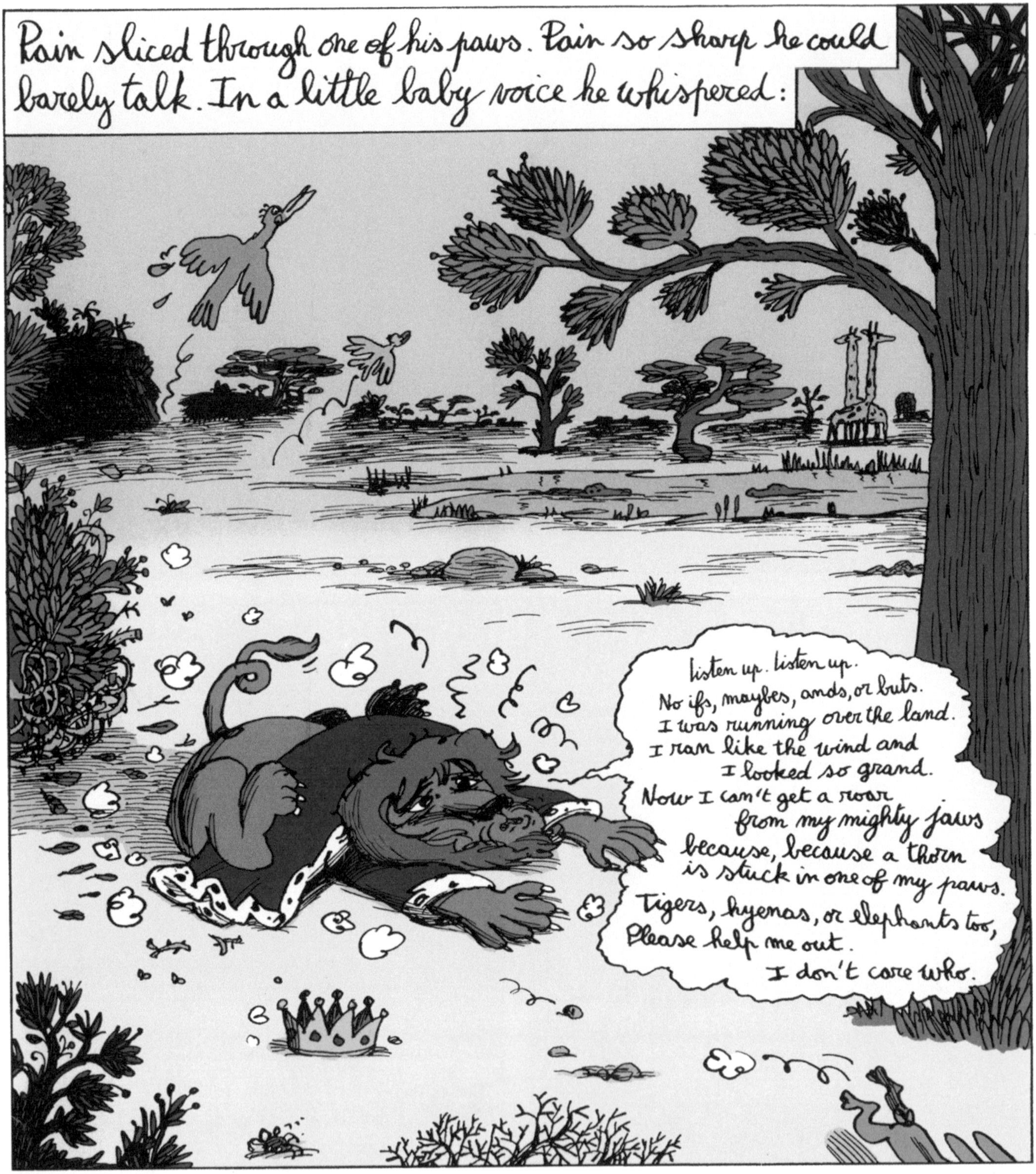
Pain sliced through one of his paws. Pain so sharp he could barely talk. In a little baby voice he whispered:
listen up. listen up.
No ifs, maybes, ands, or buts.
I was running over the land.
I ran like the wind and
I looked so grand.
Now I can't get a roar
from my mighty jaws
because, because a thorn
is stuck in one of my paws.
Tigers, hyenas, or elephants too,
Please help me out.
I don't care who.

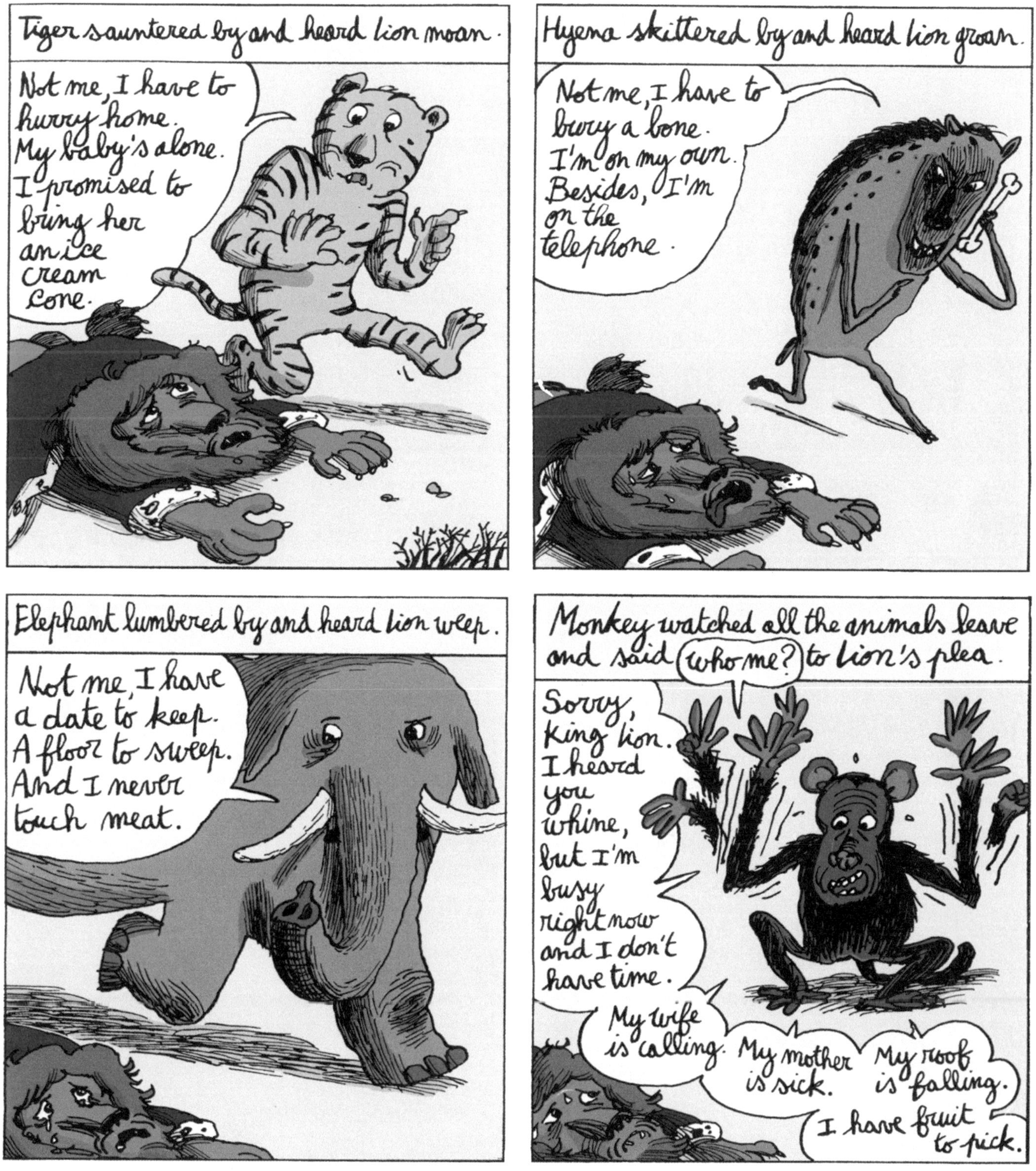
Tiger sauntered by and heard lion moan.
Not me, I have to hurry home. My baby's alone. I promised to bring her an ice cream cone.
Hyena skittered by and heard lion groan.
Not me, I have to bury a bone. I'm on my own. Besides, I'm on the telephone.
Elephant lumbered by and heard lion weep.
Not me, I have a date to keep. A floor to sweep. And I never touch meat.
Monkey watched all the animals leave and said (who me?) to lion's plea.
Sorry, King lion. I heard you whine, but I'm busy right now and I don't have time.
My wife is calling.
My mother is sick.
My roof is falling.
I have fruit to pick.

Lion sighed and tried again and again to pull the thorn from his hind paw. But he could not reach it. Not with his teeth. Not with another paw. The more he tried, the deeper the thorn sank, and the sharper the pain. He had lost all hope when he heard a squeak from the bushes nearby.

His voice was almost gone, but he was able to murmur:

listen up!

listen up!

No ifs, maybes, ands, or buts. I am the SADDEST in all the land.

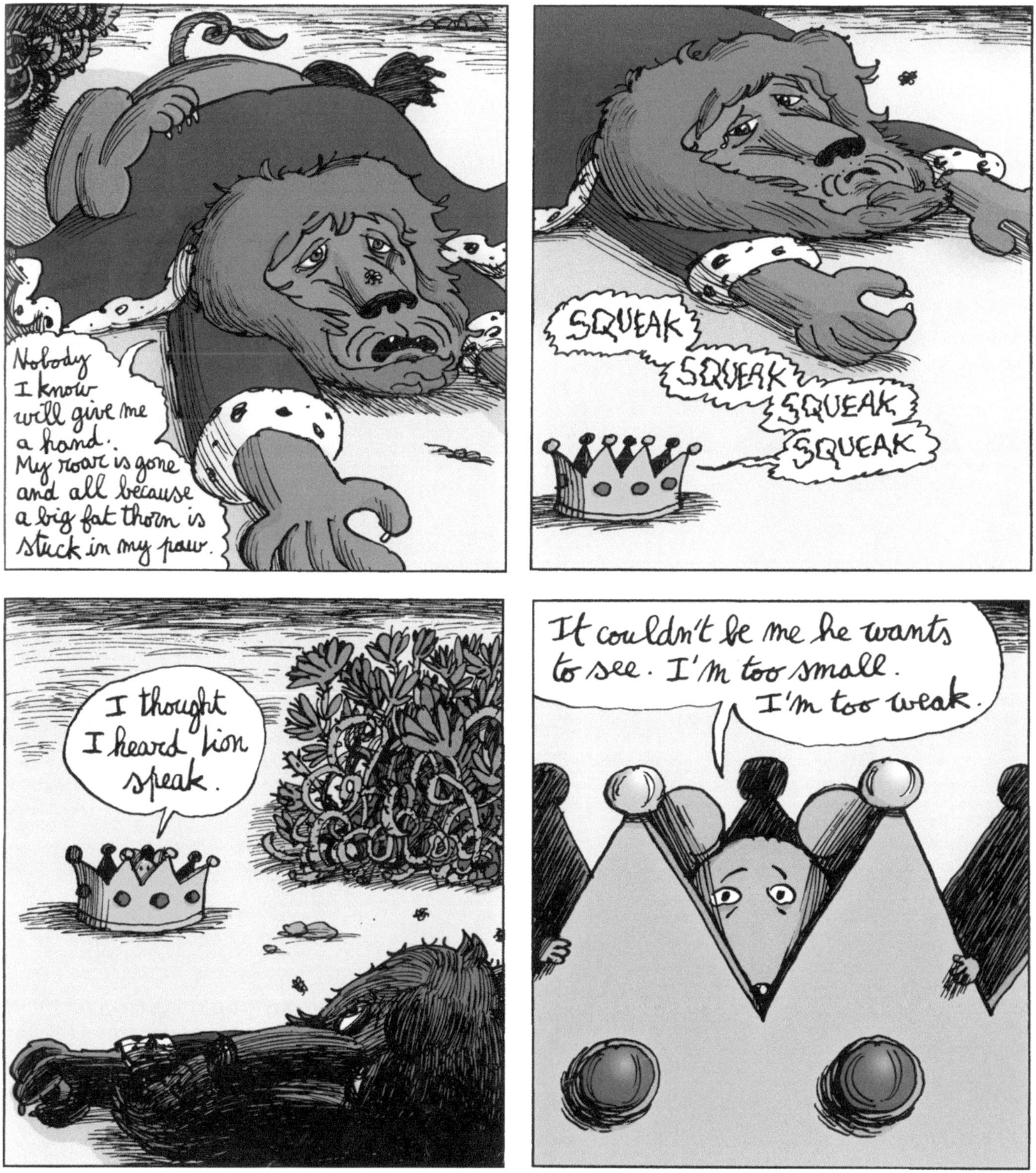
Nobody I know will give me a hand. My roar is gone and all because a big fat thorn is stuck in my paw.
SQUEAK
SQUEAK
SQUEAK
SQUEAK
I thought I heard Lion speak.
It couldn't be me he wants to see. I'm too small. I'm too weak.

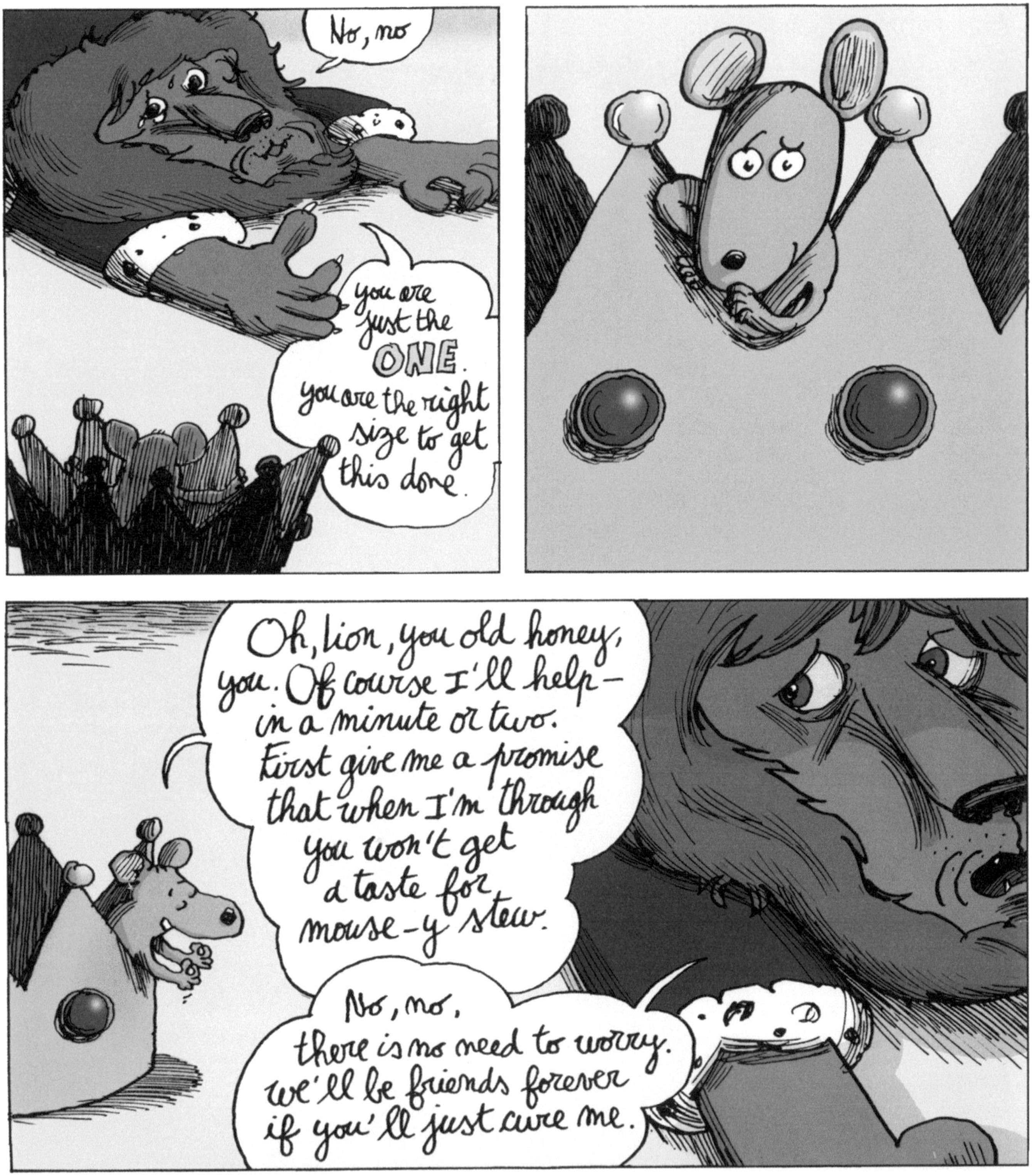
No, no
you are just the ONE. you are the right size to get this done.
Oh, Lion, you old honey, you. Of course I'll help— in a minute or two. First give me a promise that when I'm through you won't get a taste for mouse-y stew.
No, no, there is no need to worry. We'll be friends forever if you'll just cure me.

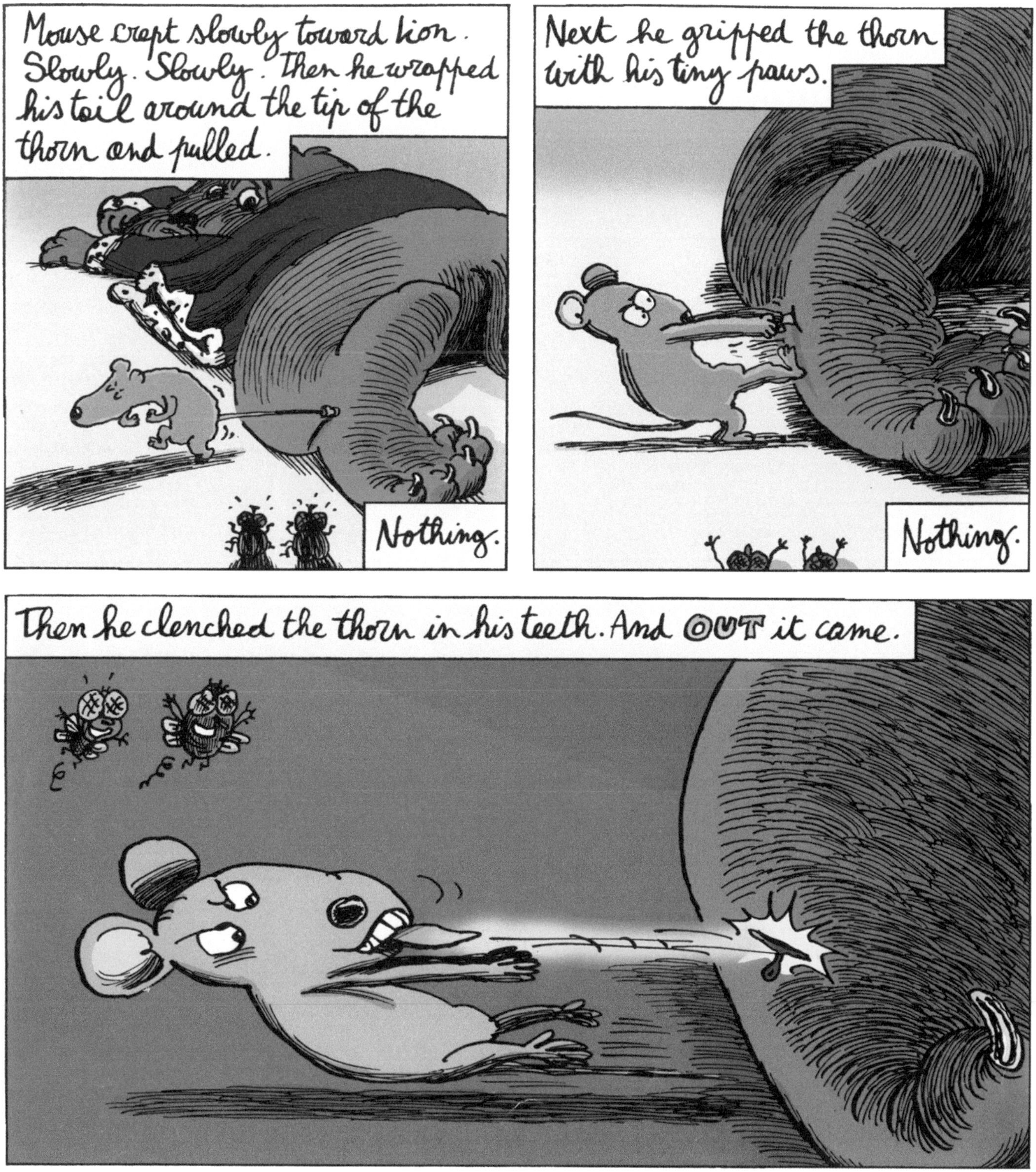
Mouse crept slowly toward Lion. Slowly. Slowly. Then he wrapped his tail around the tip of the thorn and pulled.
Nothing.
Next he gripped the thorn with his tiny paws.
Nothing.
Then he clenched the thorn in his teeth. And OUT it came.

Lion sighed with relief. Tears of gratitude moistened his eyes as he gazed at his sore and tender paw.

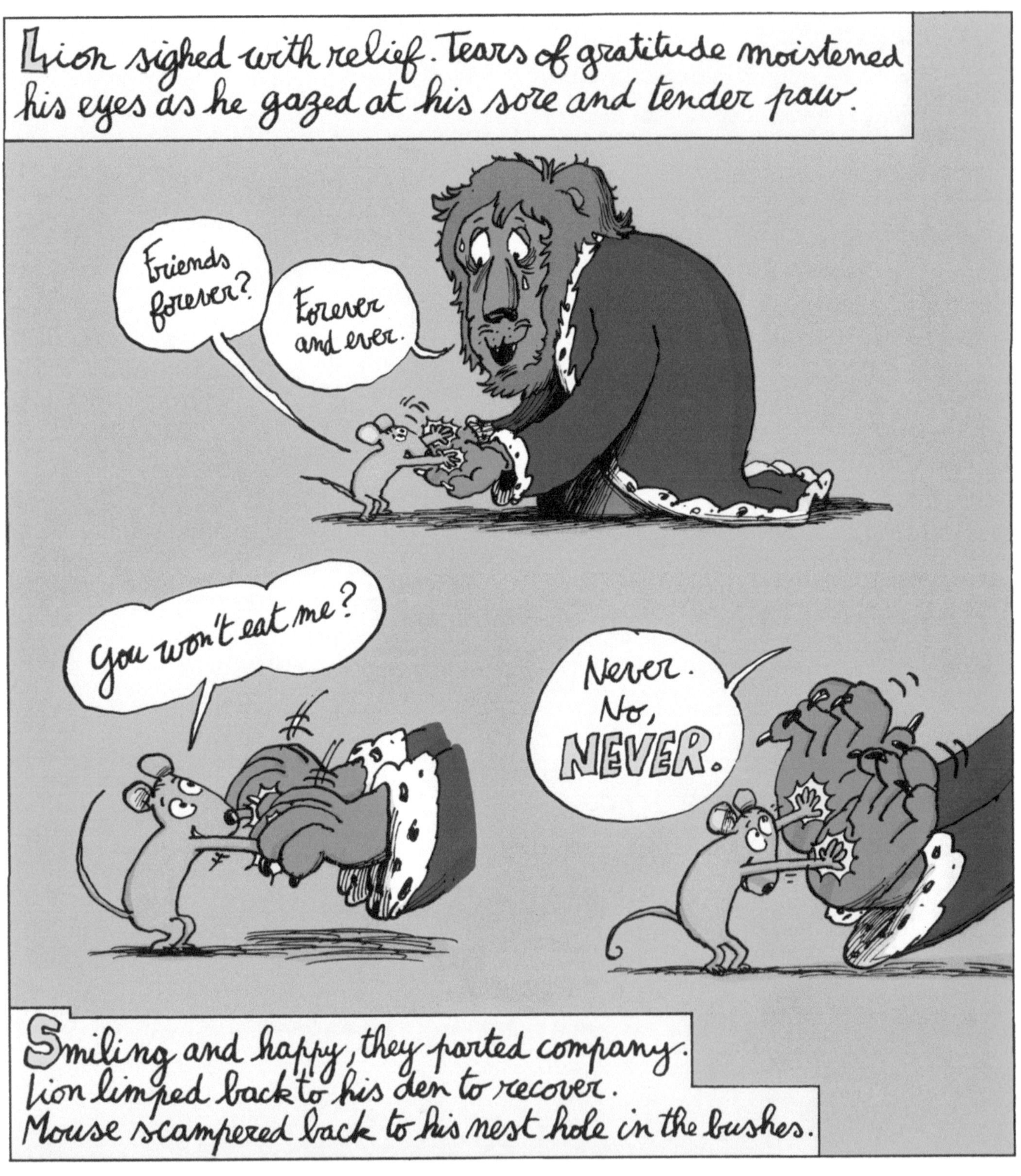
Friends forever?
Forever and ever.
You won't eat me?
Never.
No,
NEVER.

Smiling and happy, they parted company.
Lion limped back to his den to recover.
Mouse scampered back to his nest hole in the bushes.

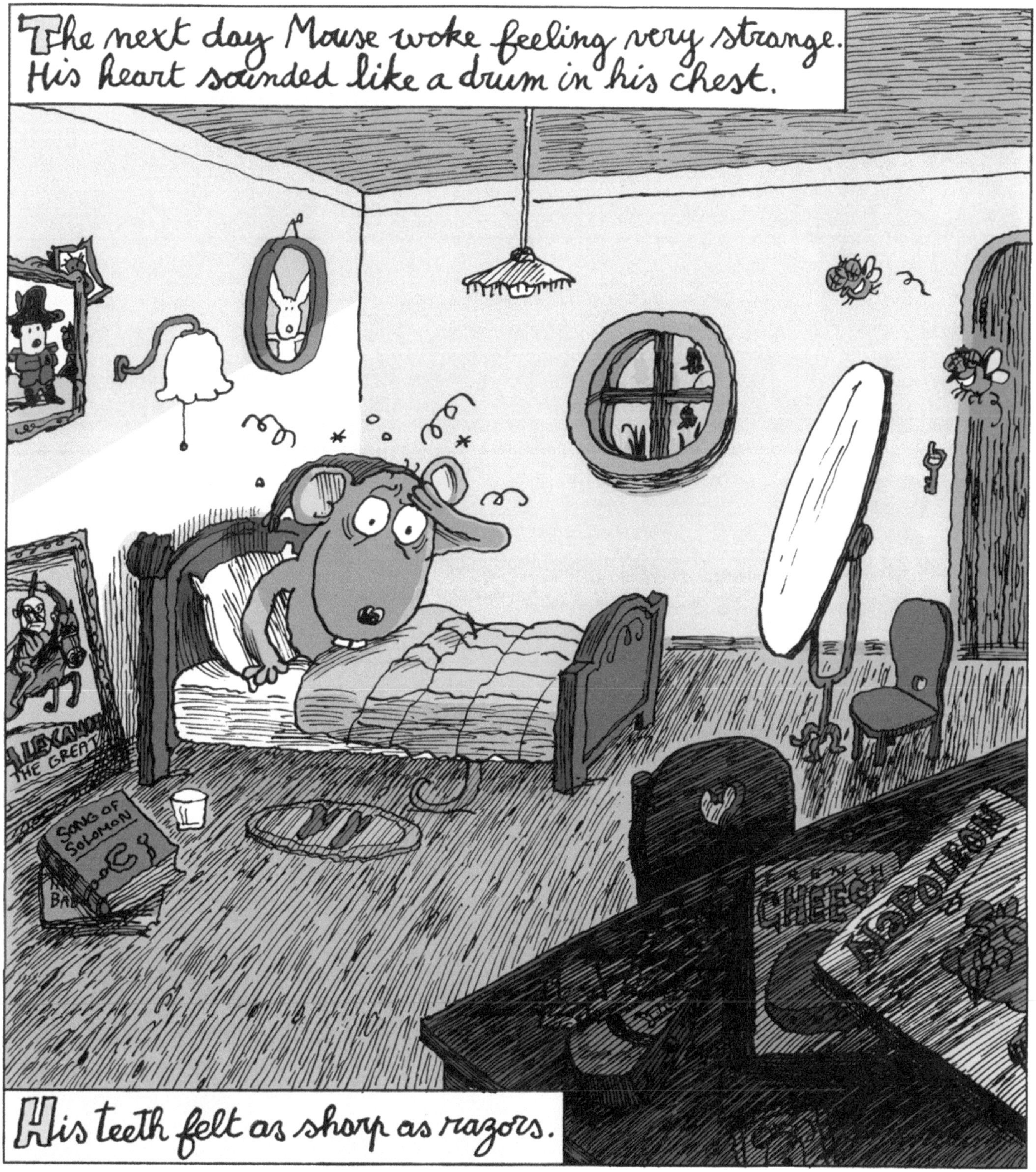
The next day Mouse woke feeling very strange. His heart sounded like a drum in his chest.
THE GREAT
SONG OF SOLOMON
NAPOLEON
His teeth felt as sharp as razors.

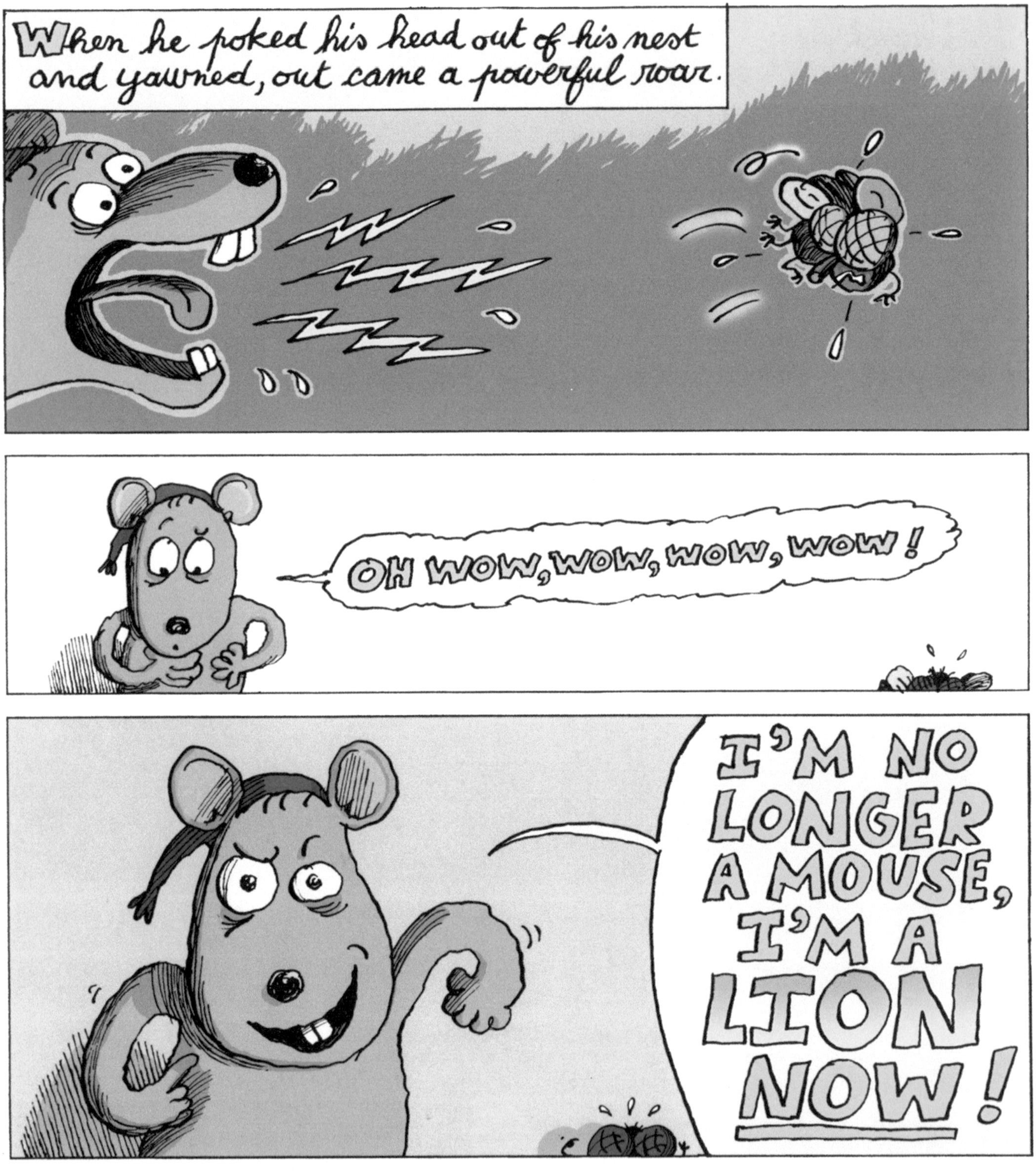
When he poked his head out of his nest and yawned, out came a powerful roar.
OH WOW, WOW, WOW, WOW!
I'M NO LONGER A MOUSE, I'M A LION NOW!

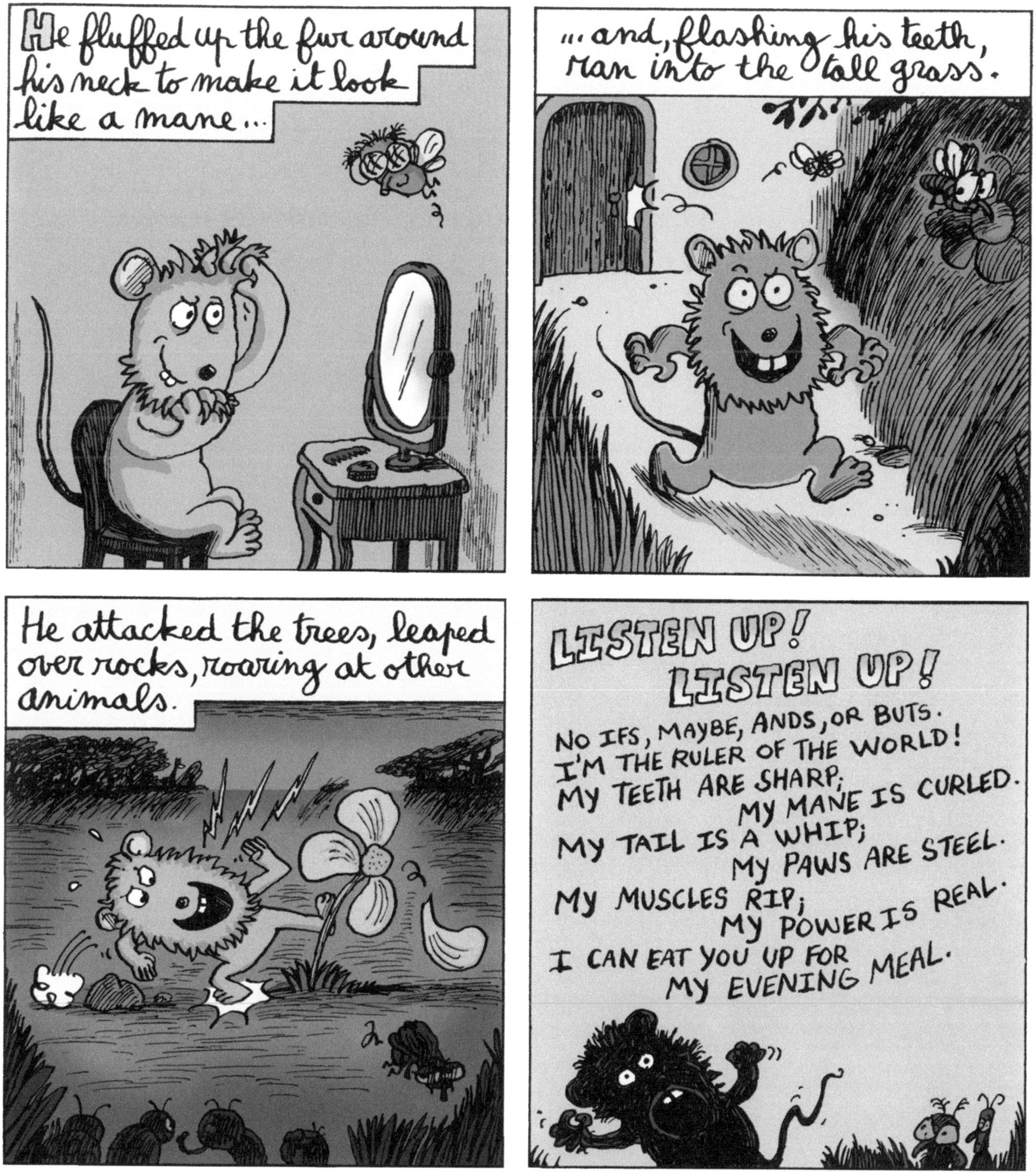
He fluffed up the fur around his neck to make it look like a mane...
...and, flashing his teeth, ran into the tall grass.
He attacked the trees, leaped over rocks, roaring at other animals.
LISTEN UP!
LISTEN UP!
NO IFS, MAYBE, ANDS, OR BUTS.
I'M THE RULER OF THE WORLD!
MY TEETH ARE SHARP;
MY MANE IS CURLED.
MY TAIL IS A WHIP;
MY PAWS ARE STEEL.
MY MUSCLES RIP;
MY POWER IS REAL.
I CAN EAT YOU UP FOR
MY EVENING MEAL.

Tiger, Hyena, and Elephant heard only a squeak coming from Mouse. Monkey wondered what made the fur around Mouse's neck stick out like spikes. He began to laugh. Tiger joined in, and then Hyena and Elephant. They all stared at Mouse and every time he squeaked or fluffed his fur, they laughed harder.

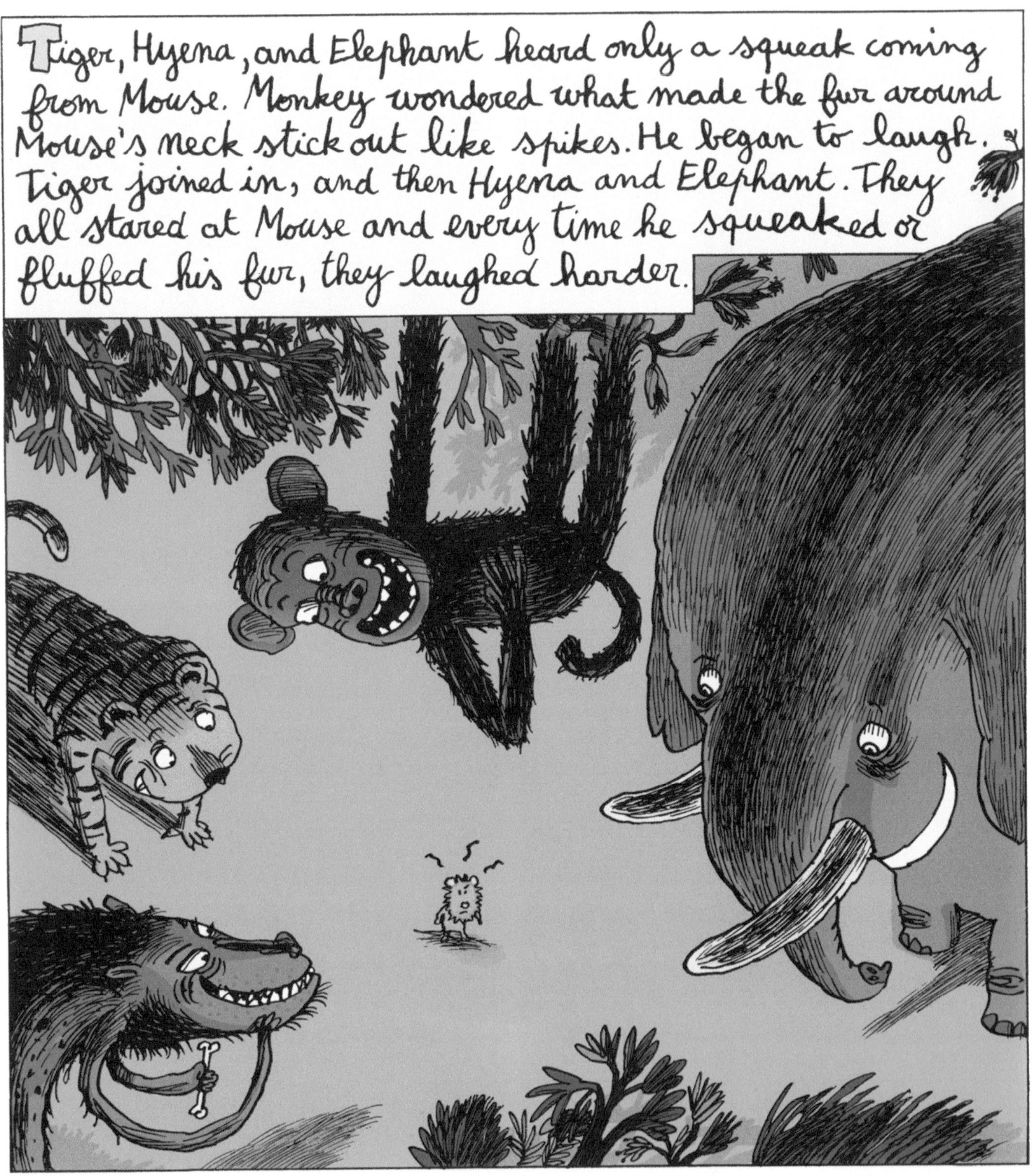

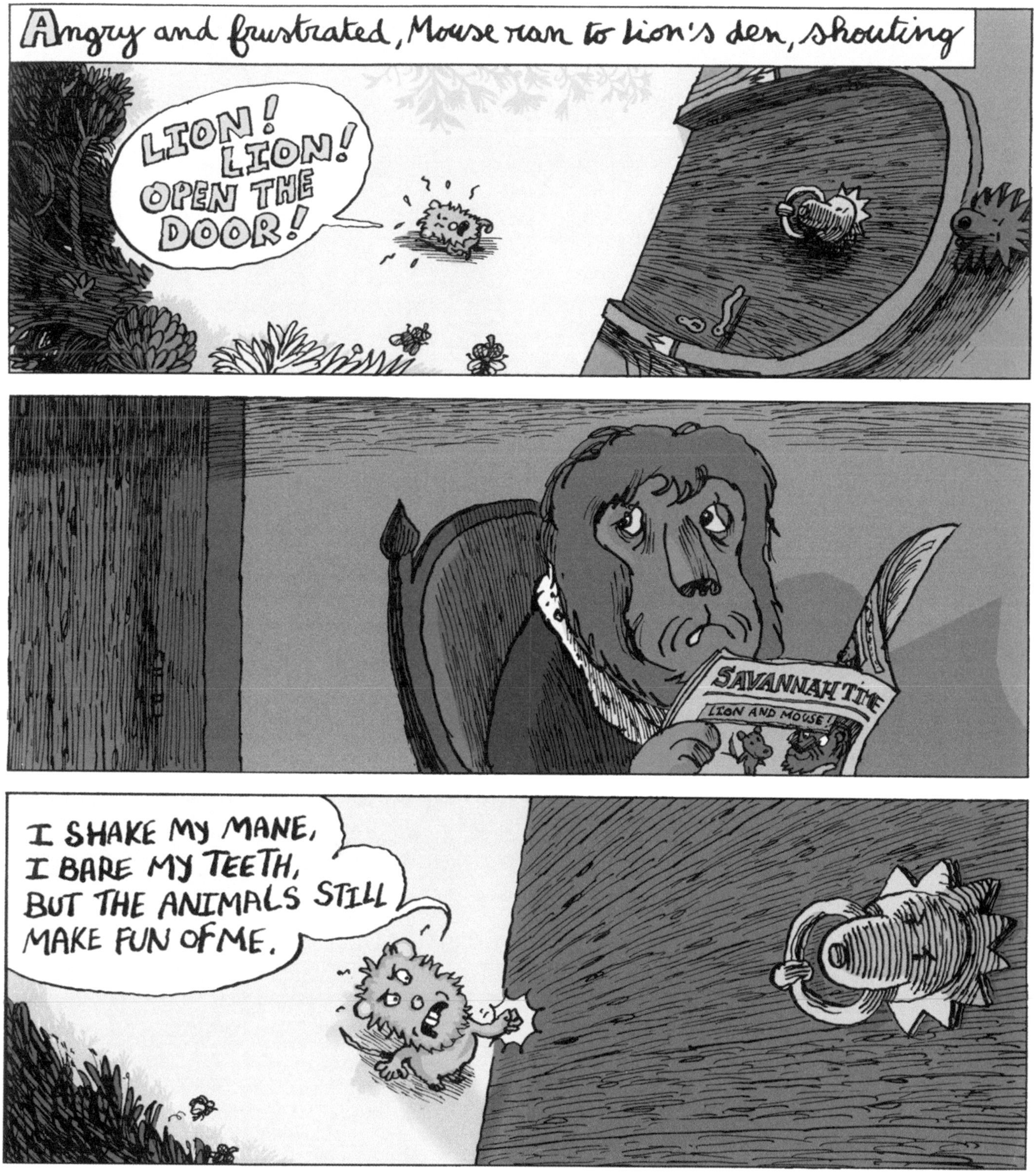
Angry and frustrated, Mouse ran to Lion's den, shouting
LION! LION! OPEN THE DOOR!
SAVANNAH TIME
LION AND MOUSE!
I SHAKE MY MANE, I BARE MY TEETH, BUT THE ANIMALS STILL MAKE FUN OF ME.

Lion rose up and ambled to the door. He was ashamed of being saved by a weak little mouse, and was hiding in his den. Now he wanted to tell Mouse to go away but he could not break his word.

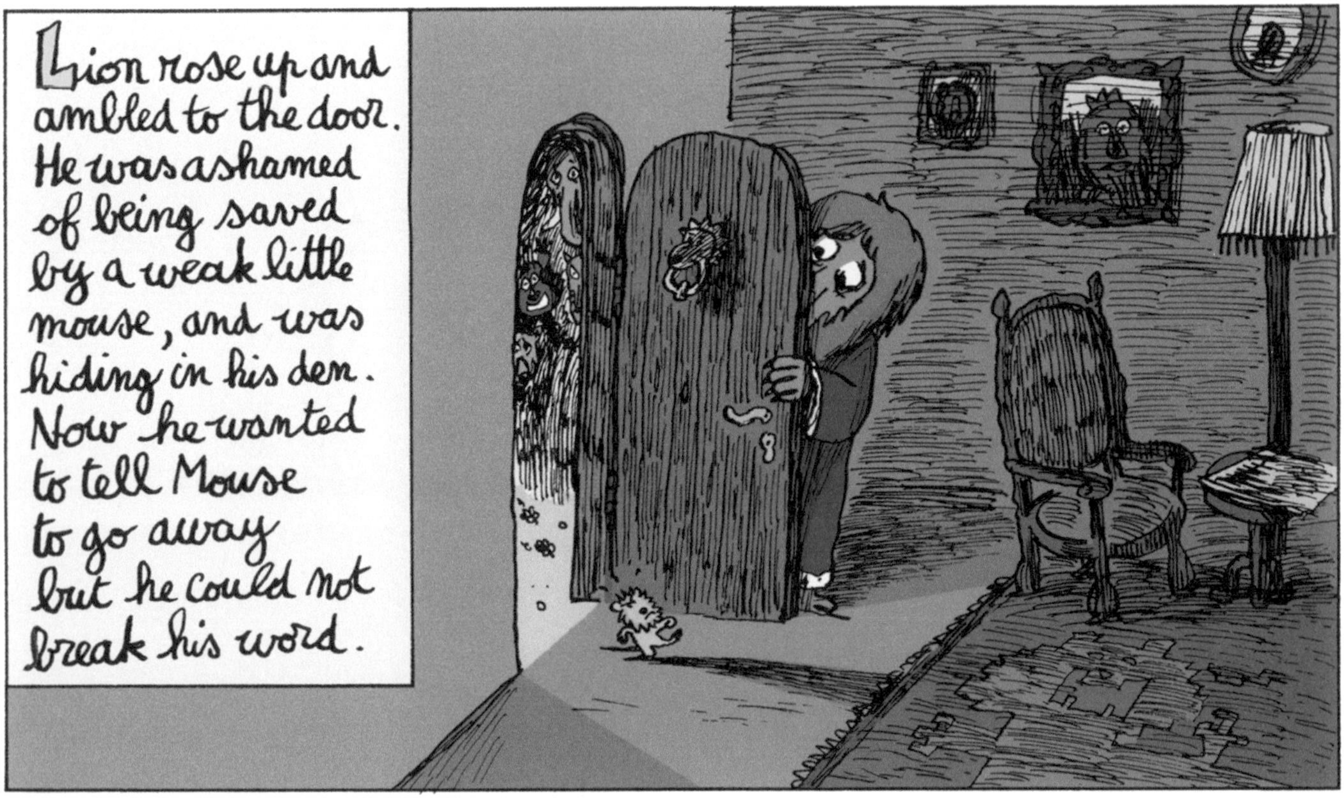

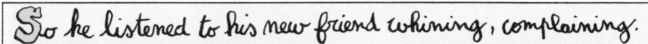

So he listened to his new friend whining, complaining.

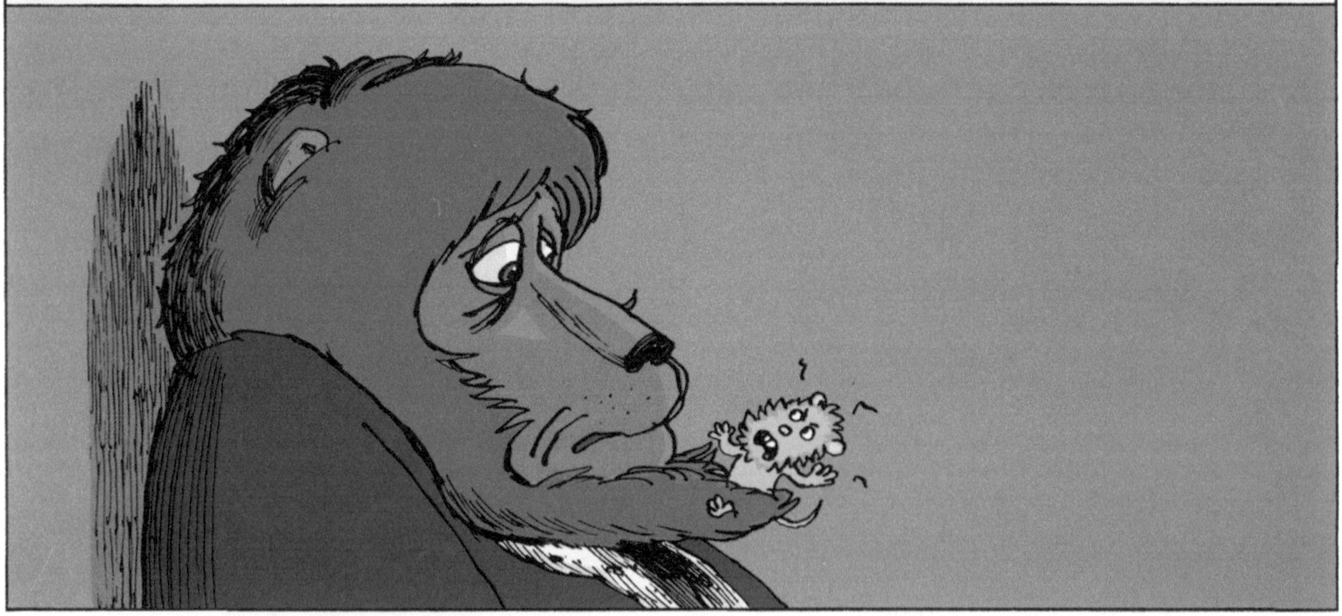

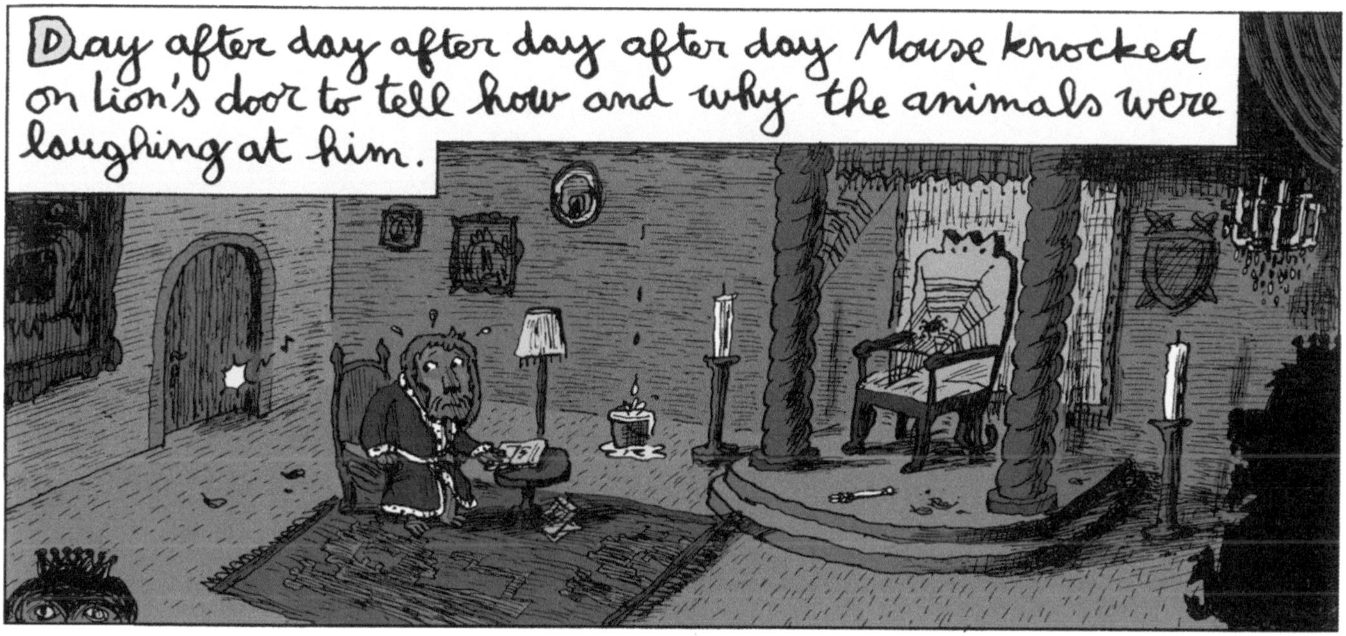
Day after day after day after day Mouse knocked on Lion's door to tell how and why the animals were laughing at him.

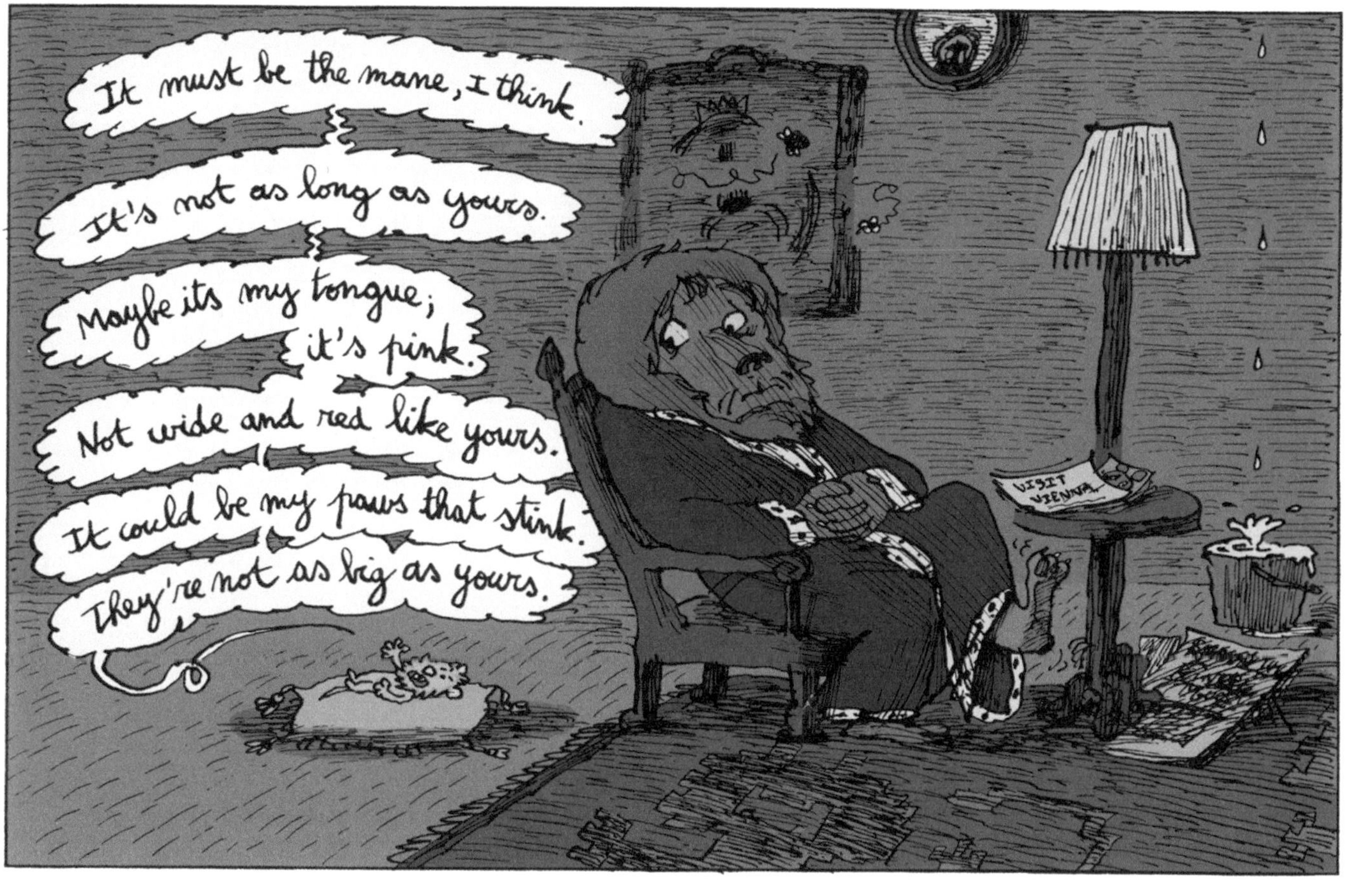
It must be the mane, I think.
It's not as long as yours.
Maybe its my tongue; it's pink.
Not wide and red like yours.
It could be my paws that stink.
They're not as big as yours.
VISIT VIENNA

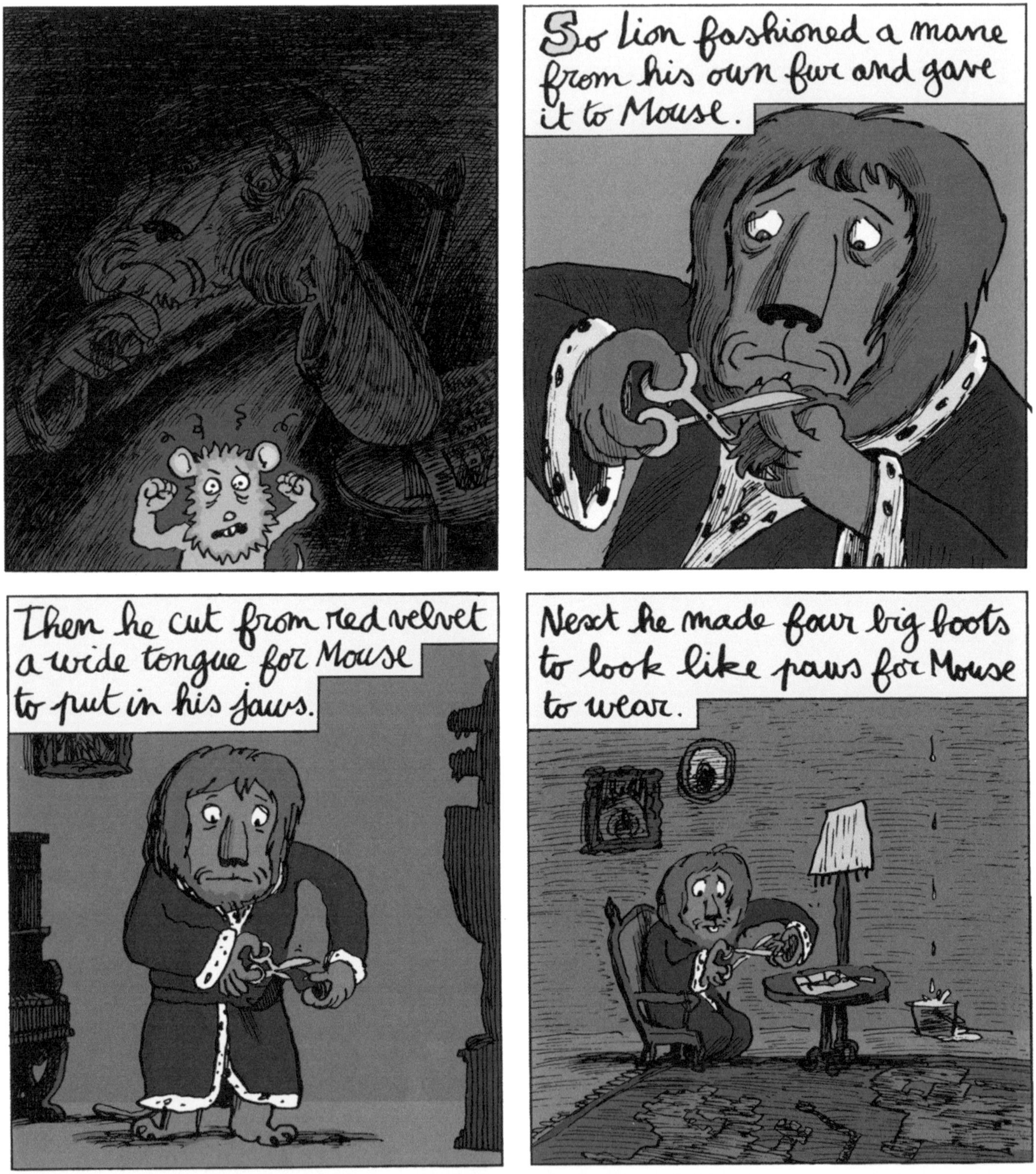
So Lion fashioned a mane from his own fur and gave it to Mouse.
Then he cut from red velvet a wide tongue for Mouse to put in his jaws.
Next he made four big boots to look like paws for Mouse to wear.

Nothing helped. Each time that Mouse appeared with a new contraption, the animals laughed even harder.

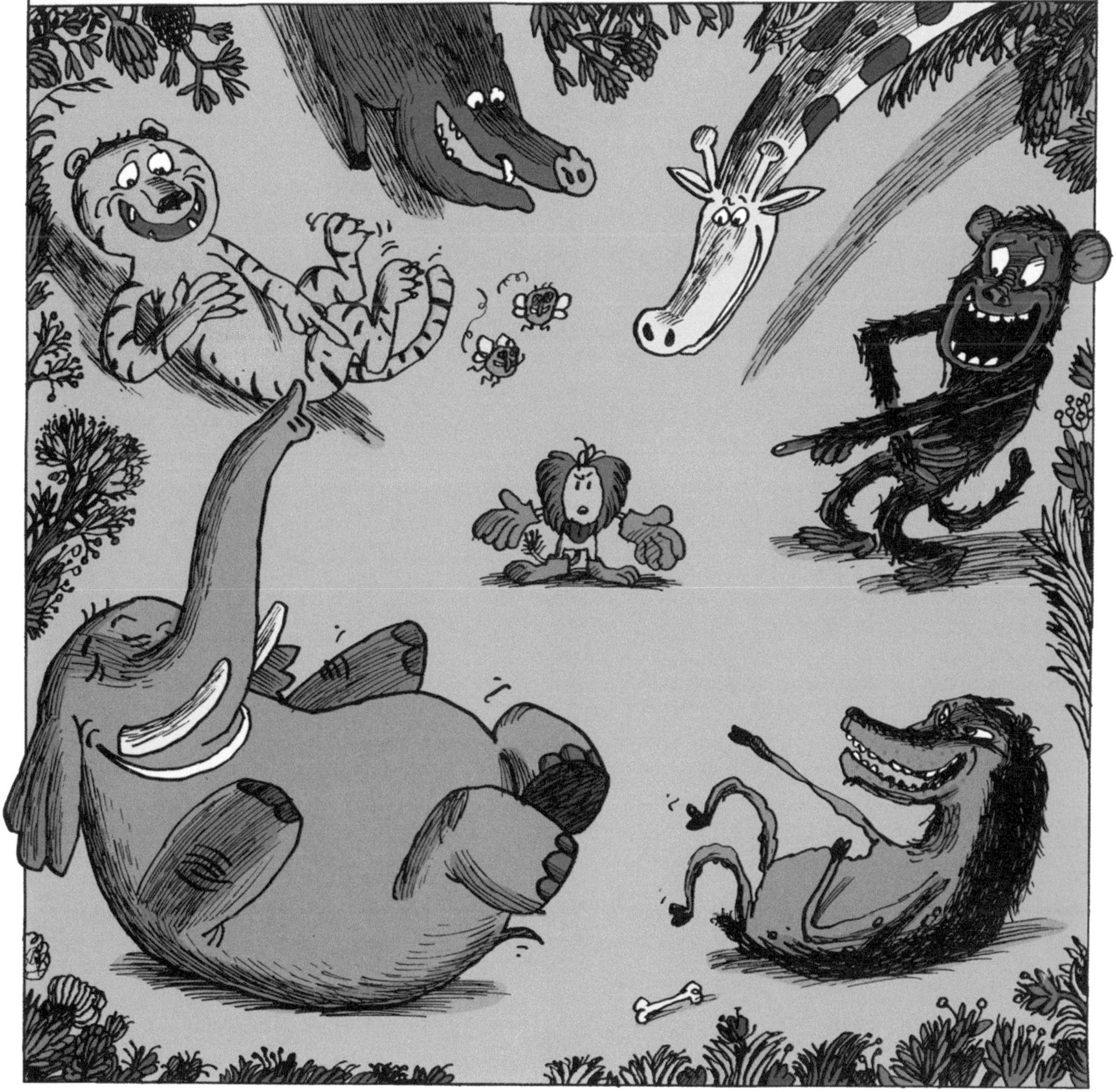

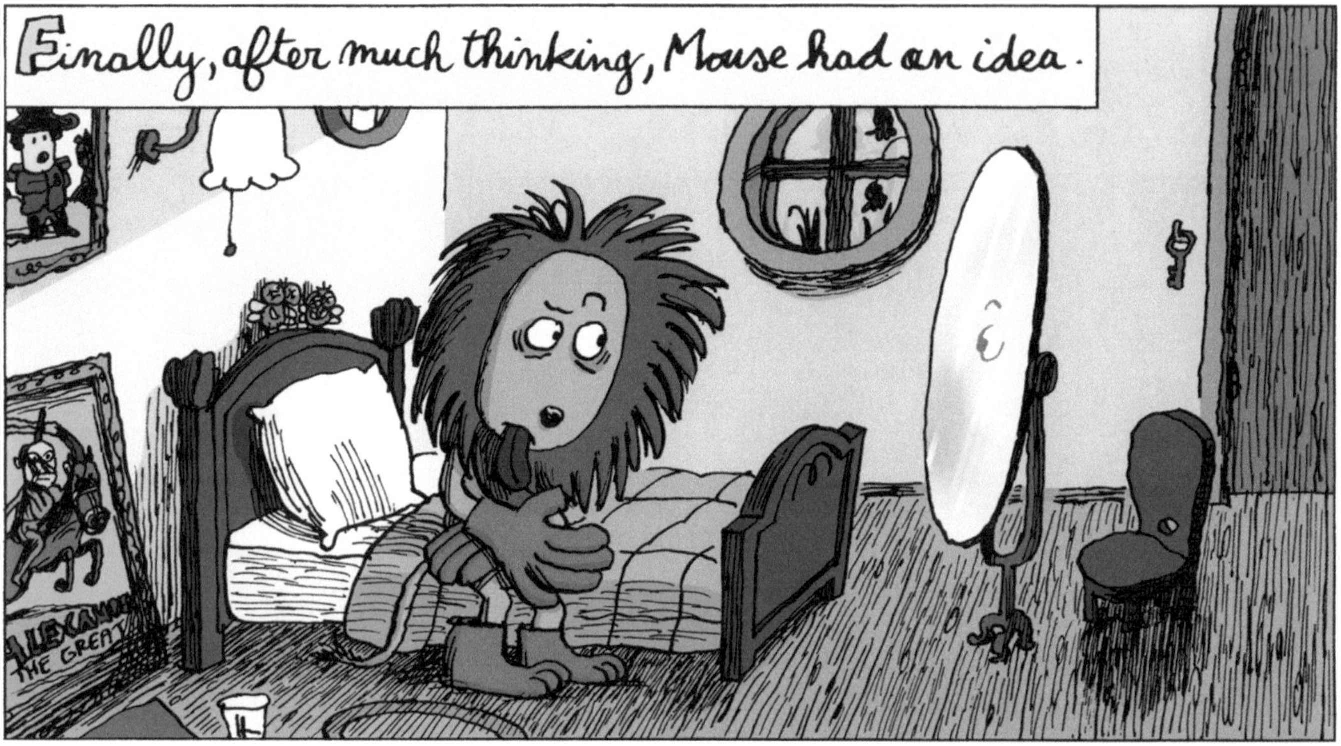
Finally, after much thinking, Mouse had an idea.
THE GREAT

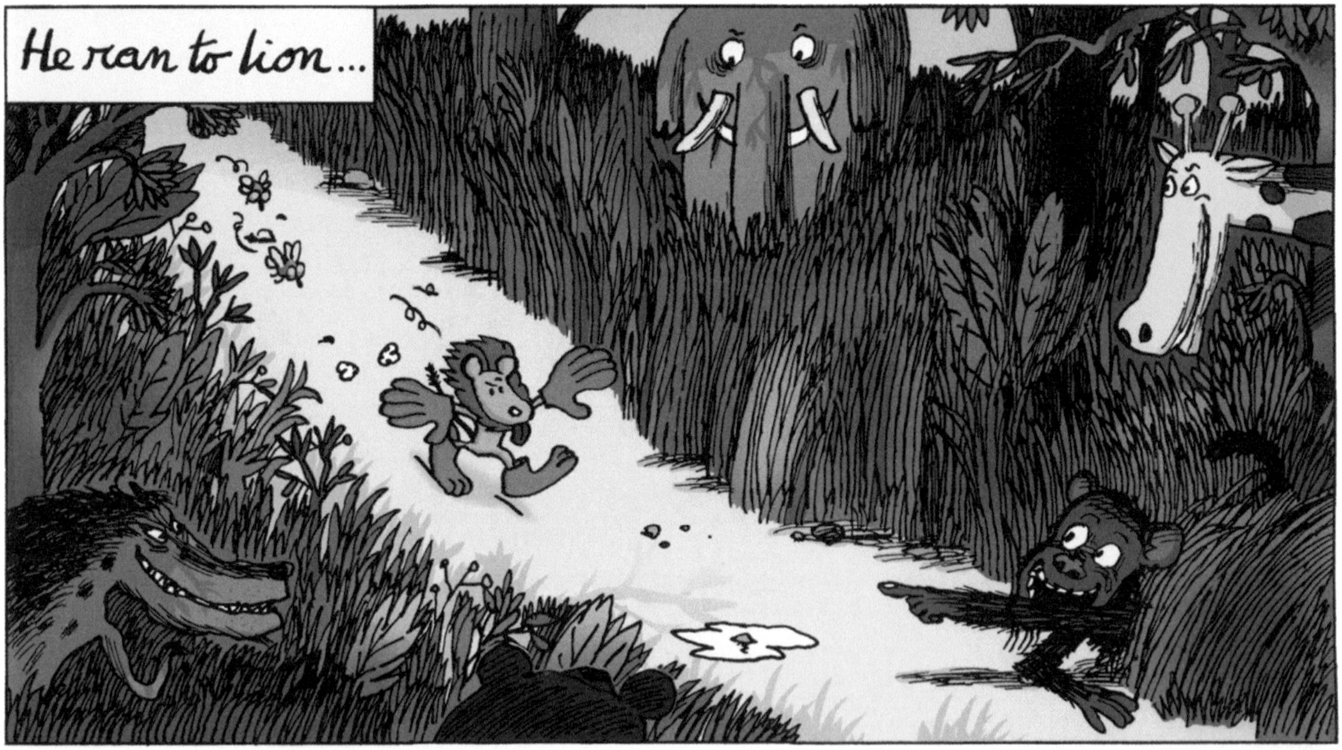
He ran to lion...

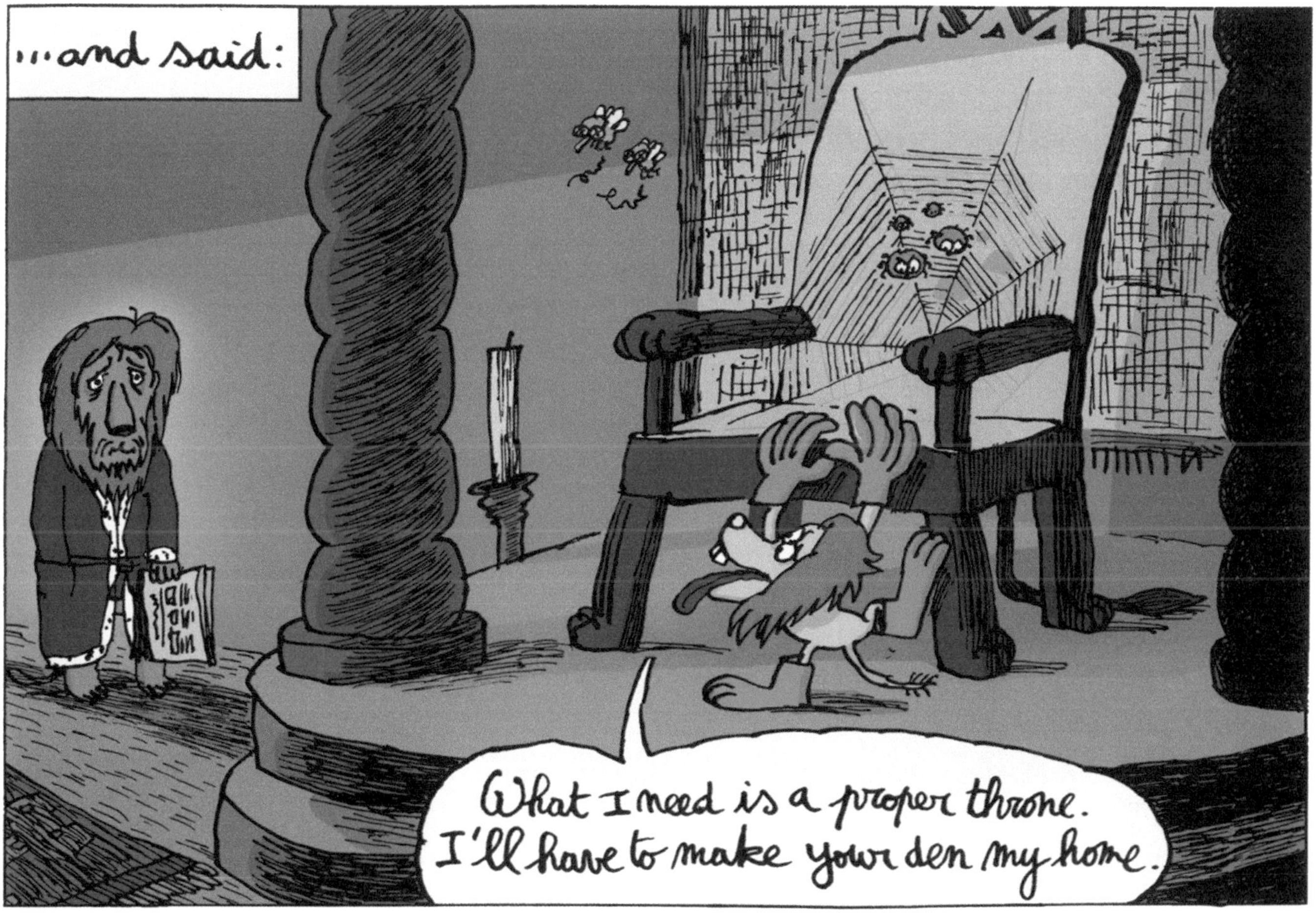
...and said:
What I need is a proper throne.
I'll have to make your den my home.

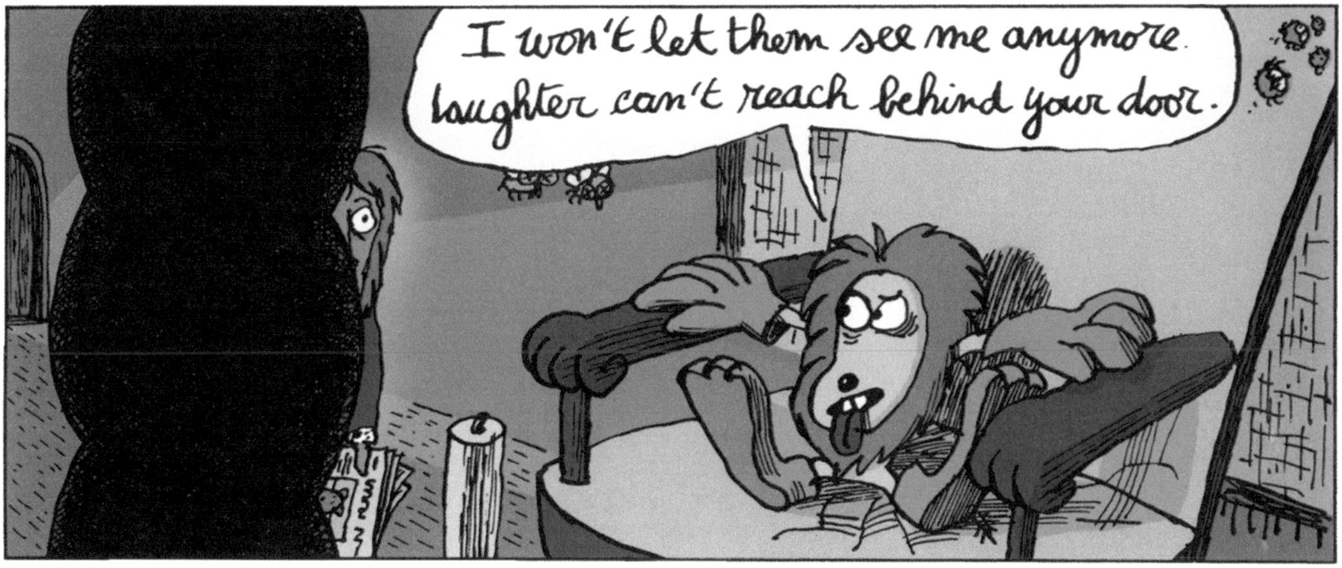
I won't let them see me anymore.
Laughter can't reach behind your door.

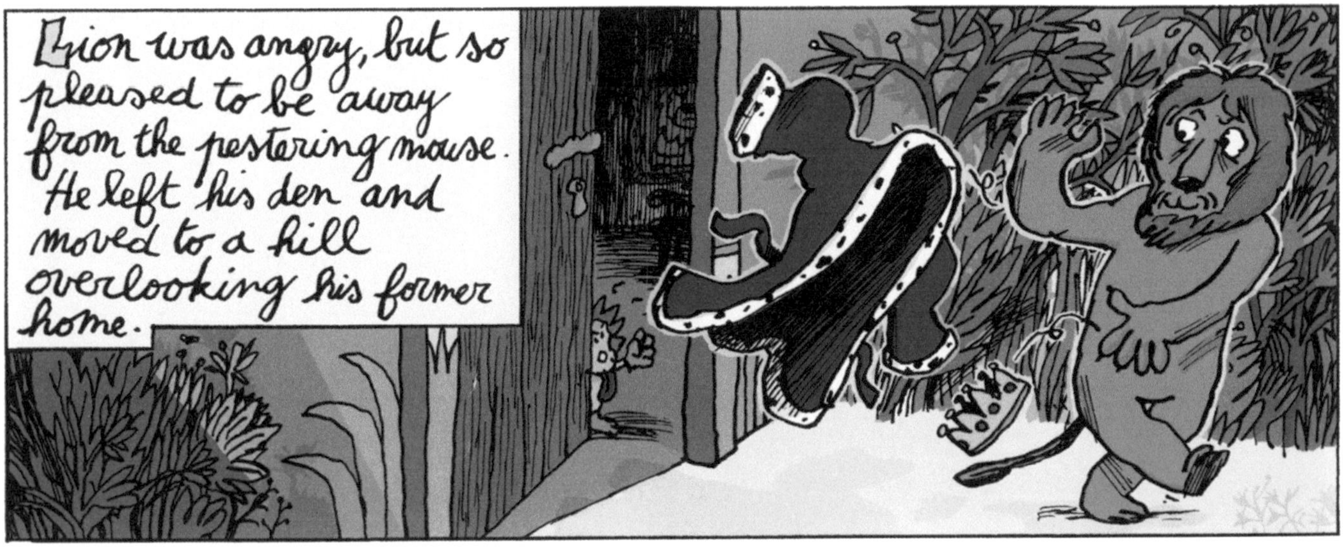
Lion was angry, but so pleased to be away from the pestering mouse. He left his den and moved to a hill overlooking his former home.

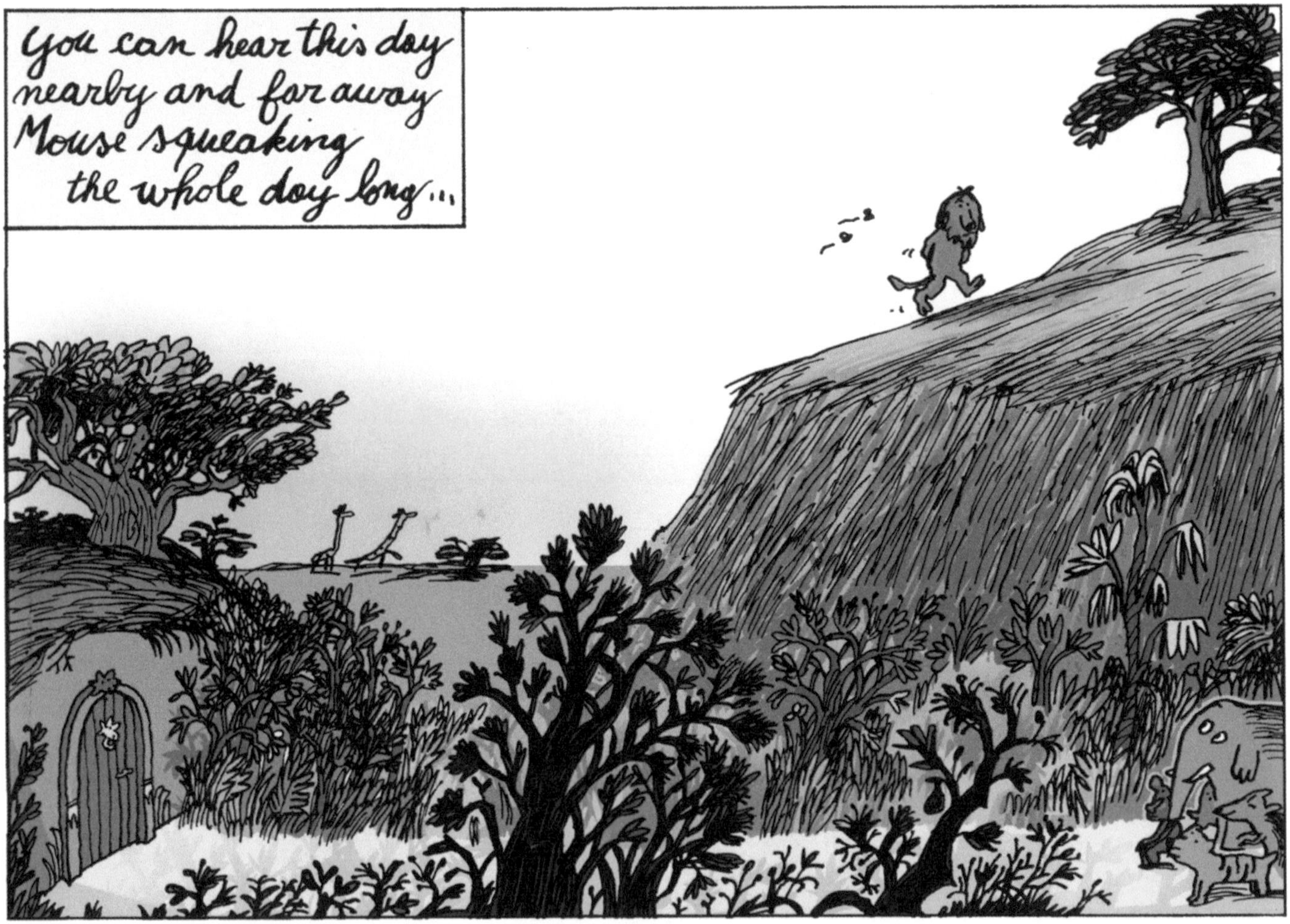
You can hear this day nearby and far away Mouse squeaking the whole day long...

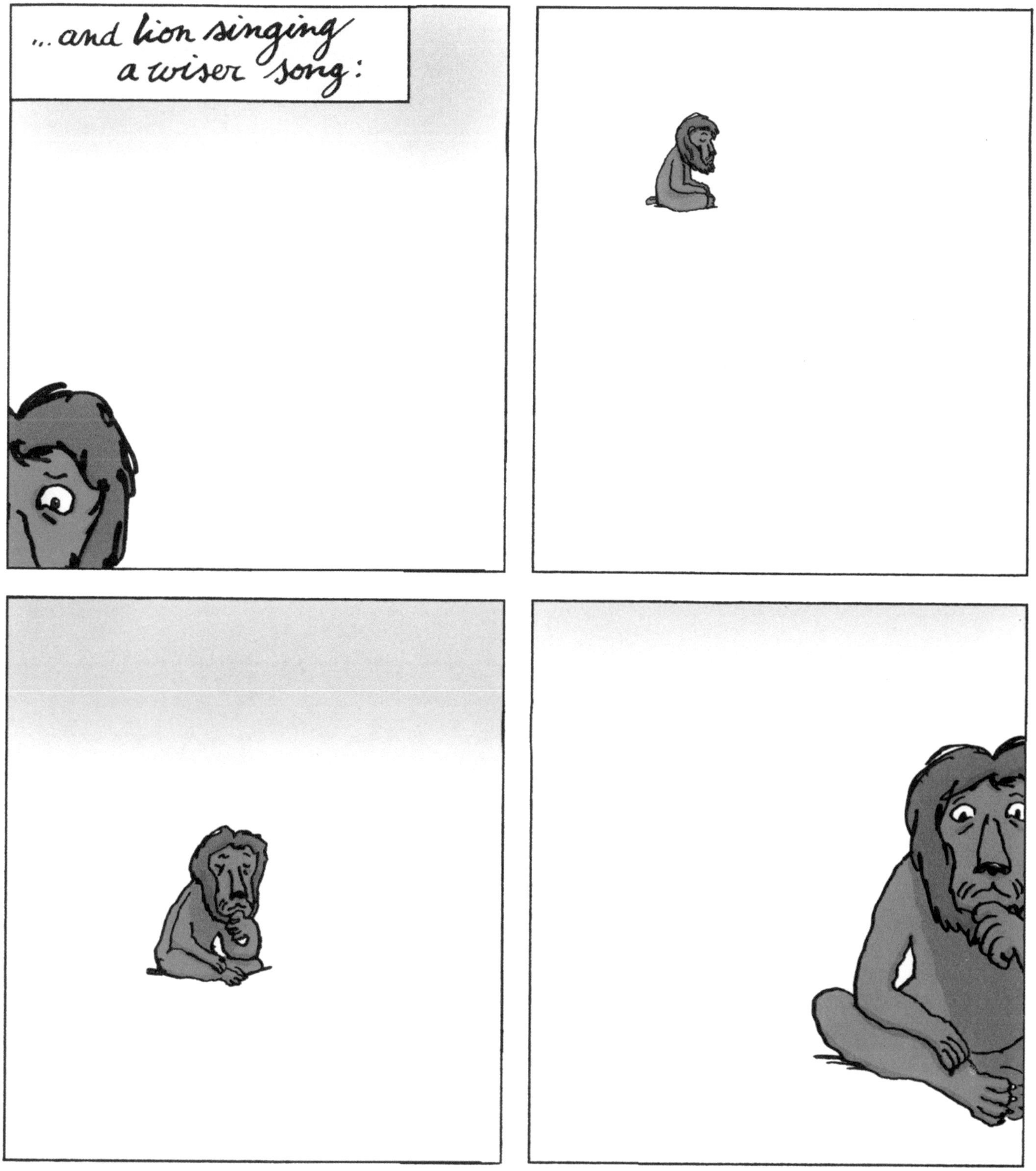
...and lion singing a wiser song:

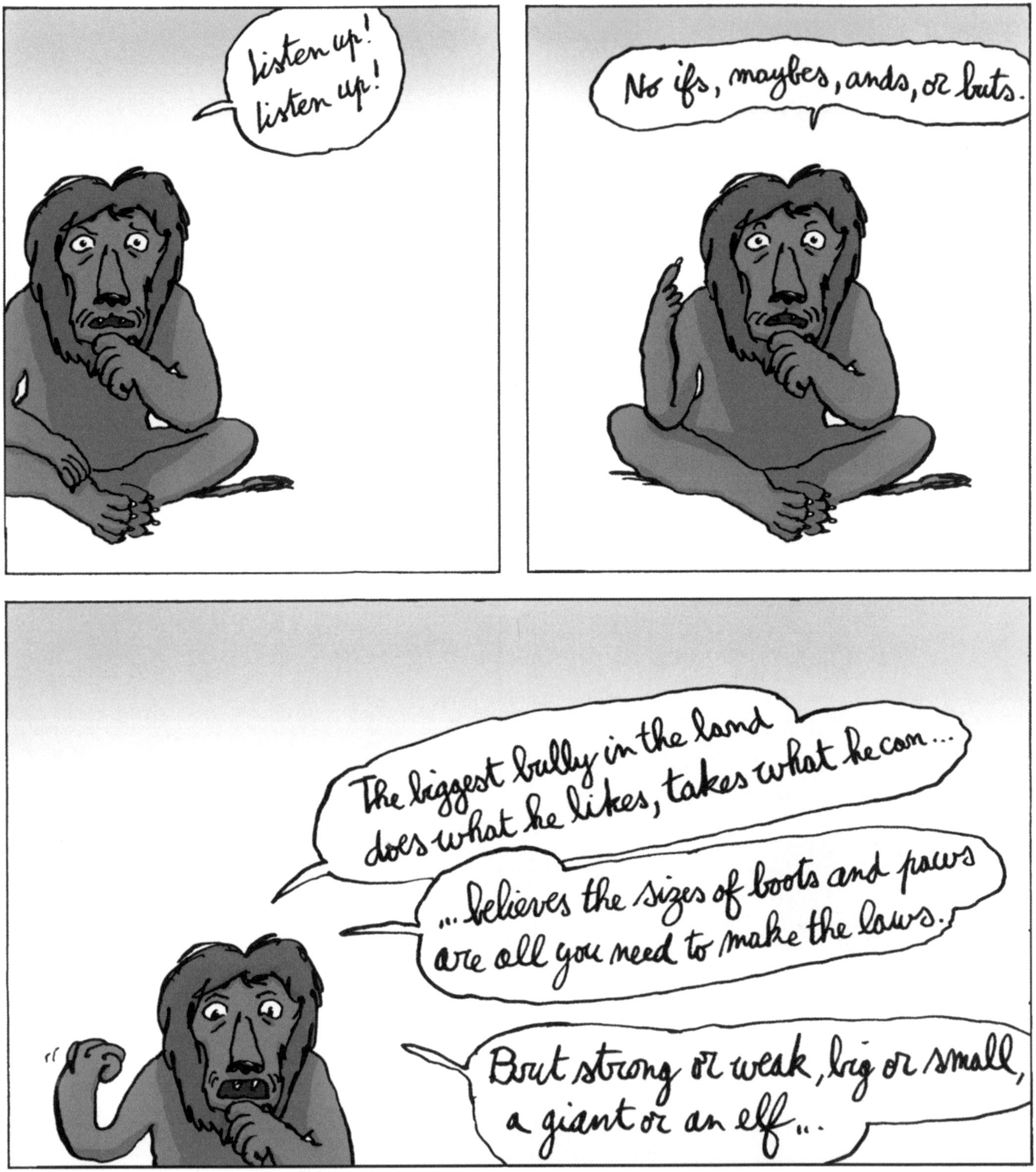
Listen up!
Listen up!
No ifs, maybes, ands, or buts.
The biggest bully in the land does what he likes, takes what he can...
...believes the sizes of boots and paws are all you need to make the laws.
But strong or weak, big or small, a giant or an elf...

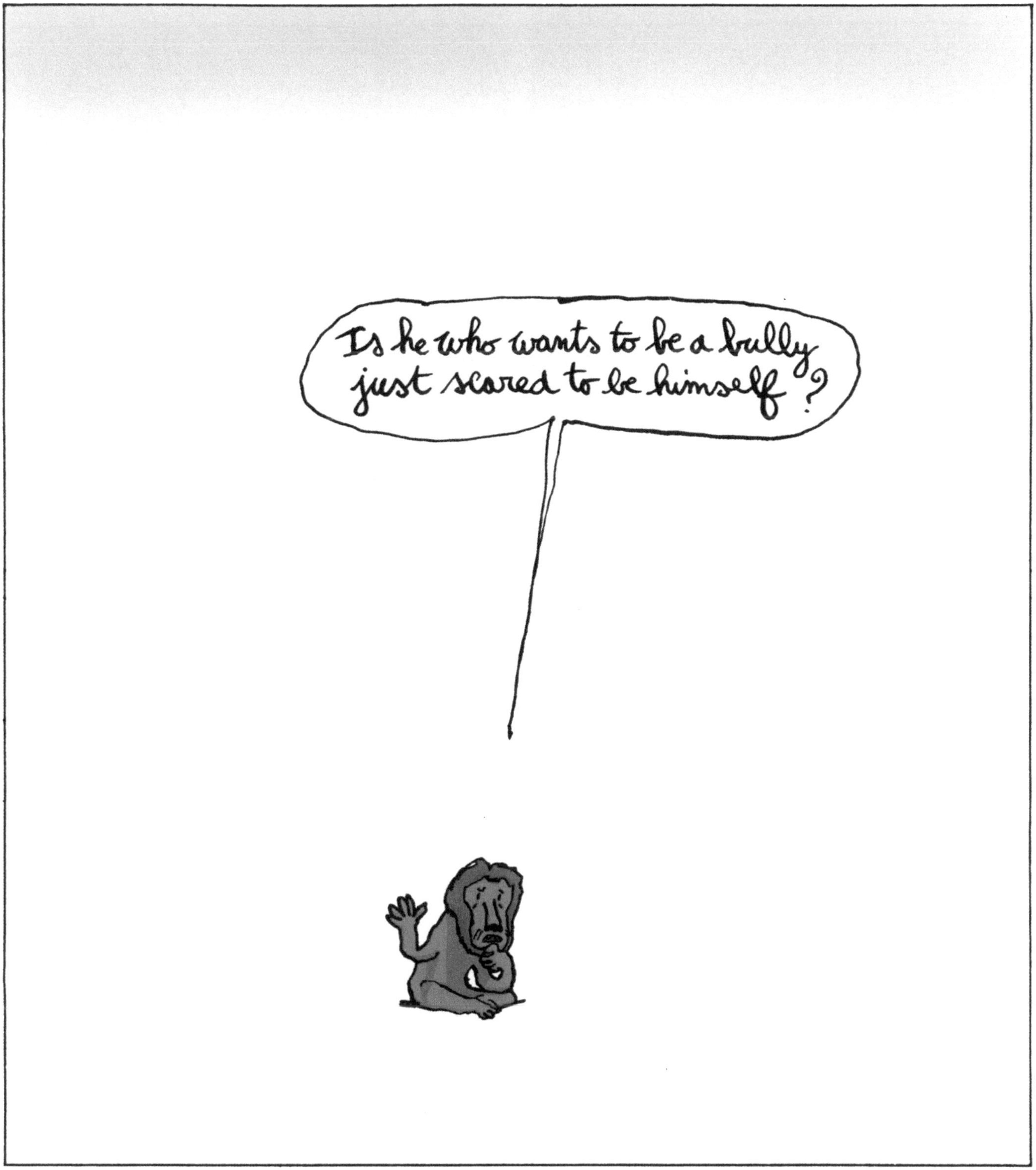
Is he who wants to be a bully just scared to be himself?

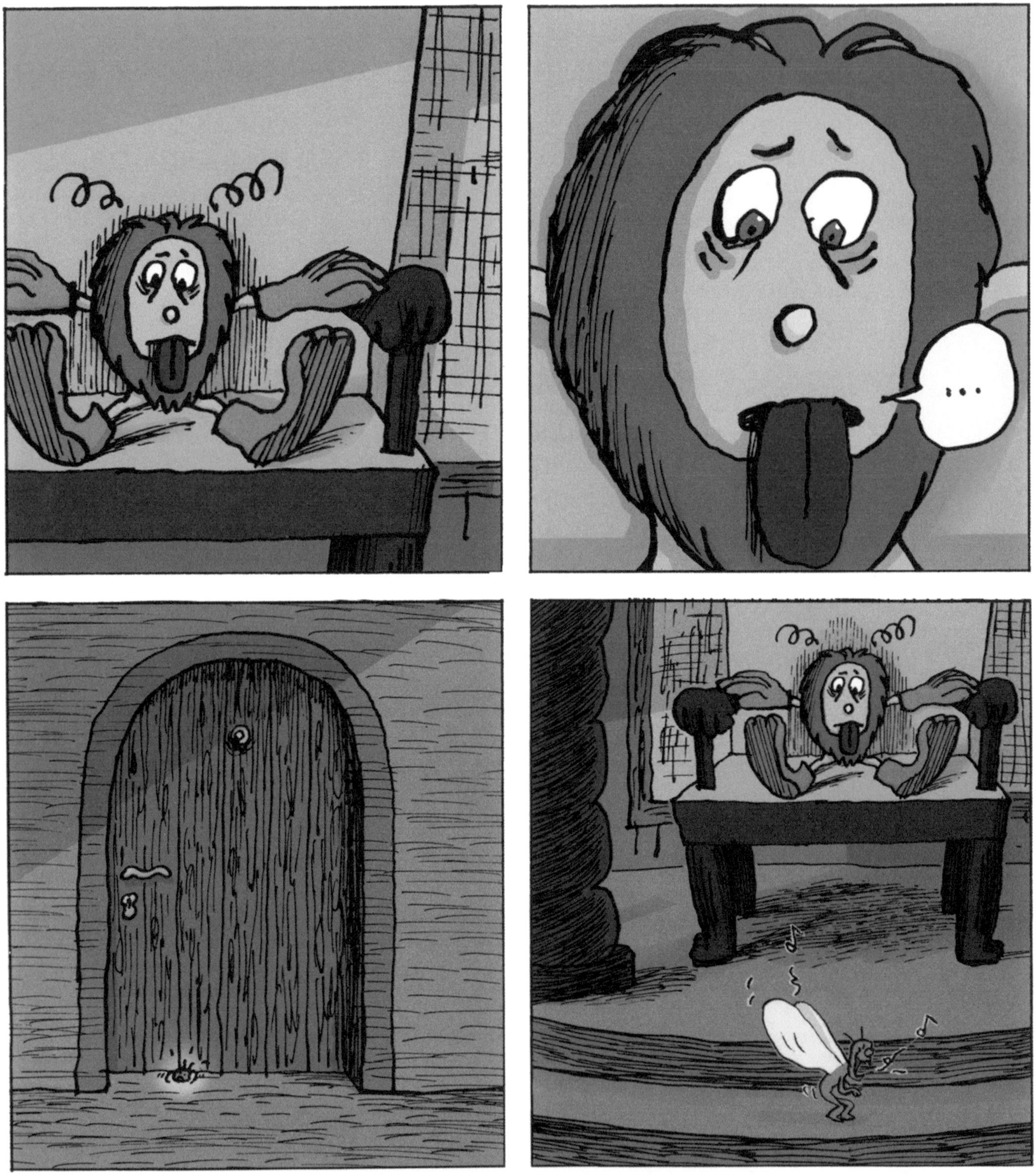
...

Printed in the United States
By Bookmasters